I0620907

AND THEN YOU'RE DEAD

A gripping action-packed thriller

DAN LATUS

Revised edition 2022
Joffe Books, London
www.joffebooks.com

First published by Robert Hale in Great Britain in 2016

This paperback edition was first published
in Great Britain in 2022

© Dan Latus 2016, 2022

This book is a work of fiction. Names, characters,
businesses, organizations, places and events are either
the product of the author's imagination or are used
fictitiously. Any resemblance to actual persons, living
or dead, events or locales is entirely coincidental.
The spelling used is British English except where fidelity to
the author's rendering of accent or dialect supersedes this.
The right of Dan Latus to be identified as author of this
work has been asserted in accordance with the Copyright,
Designs and Patents Act 1988.

Cover art by Jarmila Takač

ISBN: 978-1-80405-374-4

CHAPTER ONE

The English Borders, Northumberland, 23 September 2014

Home, he thought with a smile as he entered the village. So very good to be home.

He drove past the White Swan, and on past the paper shop and the Co-op. The chip shop was open already, he was slightly surprised to see. A bit early, surely? Town culture catching on, perhaps. 24/7. Or *Non-Stop*, as the Czechs would say. *Fish and Chips Non-Stop*!

The pothole at the junction where he turned to go up the hill was bigger than ever. Amazing the difference a few days could make. If the council didn't get their finger out soon the foundations would be washed away. Then they would have an even bigger problem than they had now, budget constraints or not.

Who was the local county councillor now anyway? He must check, and give him or her a call when he had a moment. Tell them to get Highways, or whatever they were called now after the latest reorganization, to pull their finger out.

When he had a moment! When would that be? Knowing Sam and Kyle, there wouldn't be a spare second for him from the moment he stepped through the door. He smiled again at that thought, relishing the prospect of seeing them in just a couple of minutes. There was no pleasure to match coming home to the people you loved, and who loved you right back. Nothing in the world could compare with that. He should know.

Early evening now, and growing dark. As he approached the entrance to the drive, he sighed happily and steeled himself for the rapturous welcome he would receive as mother and son held out their hands for the gifts he would surely have brought with him. It was part of the ritual of homecoming. He chuckled. He was sure they would love what he had brought them this time.

Surprisingly, the outside light above the porch door was not lit, he noted as he slid into the pool of darkness in front of the garage. He shook his head and gave a wry smile. Sam must have forgotten for once. No doubt she would be rushing around doing all those last-minute things before he arrived. Daylight would have just slipped away, its going unnoticed.

Perhaps there was a mini disaster to take care of in the kitchen? Once, the Yorkshire pudding — a dubious foreign dish, to Sam — had remained stubbornly flat, despite all her attention and best efforts. Another time the potatoes had boiled dry. Such things happened, hard as you tried to master local cuisine. You couldn't always count on everything being perfect.

Mind you, he thought fondly, with Sam things usually were. Perfect, that is. Attention to detail, persistence in the face of failure, determination to get things right were all part of her nature and her upbringing.

The front door was locked. Good! It had taken a while to drum into her head that even here you couldn't afford to leave doors open these days. There were always opportunist thieves around. Handbags, and what not, could disappear in a trice. That's how it was now. Everywhere, not just here. But it wasn't important enough to make you want to stop the world and get off. No way!

He fished out his key and opened the door.

'Hello! I'm home,' he called, as he entered the unlit hall.

The absence of light there, too, was another surprise. He closed and locked the door. Then he turned and switched on the hall light and called again, just in case they hadn't heard him. He stood, waiting, smiling and expectant. Then he frowned. There had been no answering call. More than that, the house was so quiet. Too quiet.

He made his way through to the kitchen, which was also in darkness. He switched on the light, half-expecting to be jumped on by his excited son, eager to surprise him. Nothing happened. There was nobody here. No smell of cooking, either. The cooker was lifeless, and held no pans or dishes. Both hob and oven felt quite cold when he touched them.

He frowned and walked back to the foot of the stairs, which were also in darkness.

'Sam! Kyle! I'm home.'

Again, no reply.

He shook his head, puzzled, and made his way upstairs to check. A frisson of anxiety ran through his mind as he confirmed that his son and wife were not upstairs, either. In fact, they were not in the house. And no note had been left to explain why.

Now he frowned with worry. It wasn't like Sam to be absent when he was expected home. Something had happened, obviously. Some sort of emergency, perhaps? Perhaps.

Yet everything had been fine earlier that day when he had last called. No hint of a problem, here or anywhere else, either. Still . . . something had happened. Obviously. What, though?

He hesitated at the foot of the stairs, uneasy and concerned, and wondering what to do for the best. Nothing like this had ever happened before, even though he had never quite got over his fear that it might. For a long time he had even half-expected it, but not in recent years.

CHAPTER TWO

Sam's car was still in the garage. He frowned and closed the garage door. What did that mean? They hadn't needed the car? Probably. They must just have gone somewhere in the village.

So they would be back soon, no doubt full of apologies for not having been here when he arrived. He smiled with relief and shook his head. How stupid he had been to worry prematurely.

Back in the house, he switched on more lights to make the place look normal and welcoming. Then he went through to the kitchen to make himself a cup of coffee.

At least everything was in order here, as usual, he thought, glancing around. That was one thing you couldn't fault Sam on. She was unbelievably tidy and orderly. If you took something off, he could hear her saying, you hang it up. If you finished with something, you put it away. As much as possible, she kept things tidy and organized, to everyone's advantage. Lesson learned early in an untidy life.

He shook his head affectionately. Sam had an uphill battle with their son in that respect. Kyle was not one of nature's tidy people. He seemed to have inherited his father's genes. Wherever he went, Kyle left chaos like a scattergun.

On impulse, he went back upstairs and checked the master bedroom and his son's room. Both were immaculate. He frowned. So that meant Kyle had not been back here from school. Sam must have met him in the village and gone somewhere from there with him.

The doctor's? Possibly, but she hadn't said anything about either of them having an appointment or feeling unwell when he spoke to her. Somewhere else, then. Shopping, perhaps? The Co-op? But they should have been back by now, if that was where they had gone.

He returned to the kitchen and finished making his coffee. Then he stood near the sink with it, staring out through the window into the gathering darkness beyond, wishing they were here with him. The house was so empty without them, and he had been looking forward so much to them being here when he arrived.

He didn't stay there for long. It was no good. He couldn't fool himself. He didn't even finish the cup of coffee. With an impatient sigh, he poured what was left into the sink and washed it away. He rinsed the cup and put it in the rack. Then he collected an outdoor jacket from the cupboard in the hall and headed for his car. He was going to look for them.

They were not in the Co-op or the newsagents. They were not in the tea shop, either, which in any case was empty by now. Nor were they in any of the other little shops that were still open. And they were not on the street. That seemed to leave the GP's surgery.

But they were not there, either. The receptionist added that they hadn't been in earlier, and hadn't had an appointment anyway. She was sorry. She just hadn't seen them. He thanked her and left.

At the Church of England Primary School, all the lights were ablaze, but inside he found only a couple of cleaners, women he didn't know.

'There's just us here now,' a kindly, older woman, said. 'And we'll be finished soon ourselves.'

'I thought my wife and son might be here,' he said vaguely. 'I could have given them a lift home.'

The woman smiled her regrets for his wasted journey. He thanked her and turned away.

What did that leave? Friends and acquaintances, he supposed. Maybe they had visited someone, possibly someone in the midst of a domestic crisis. A child or an older person had been rushed to hospital, perhaps, and Sam had been asked to look after things for an hour or two. It could happen. It had happened. Young mothers were often called upon to help at such times.

But he would have expected her to leave a message if she had gone somewhere like that. The absence of a message, a note — anything! — worried him. It worried him a lot. He couldn't deny it.

He decided the best thing he could do now was return home and ring around a few people. Someone must know where they were.

First he phoned the school secretary, a woman he knew his wife liked and respected.

'Jack Tait here, Mrs Cummings. I believe you know my wife — and my son, Kyle?'

'Good evening, Mr Tait. Yes, of course I know them. Is there something I can help you with?'

'I wondered if you knew if Kyle was in school today.'

'I believe so, yes.' There was a pause. Then: 'Why do you ask?'

He hesitated for a moment but he knew he had no choice now. He had to go on.

'I've just returned from a business trip. I expected to find my wife and Kyle at home but they're not there. So I wondered if there had been some sort of family emergency, perhaps to do with Kyle.'

'Well, nothing out of the ordinary has happened to my knowledge, Mr Tait, and I'm sure I would have heard if it had. I'll check with Mrs Roberts, Kyle's class teacher, but I'm sure he was in school as normal. If he wasn't, I'll let you know.'

He thanked her and ended the call.

Next, he phoned the mother of a little boy he knew Kyle played with sometimes.

'Hello, Chris. Jack Tait here. You haven't got Kyle with you, by any chance?'

'Hi, Jack! No, he's not here. Should he be?'

Again he hesitated, unsure how much he wanted to confide to a casual acquaintance. He didn't want to give tongues an opportunity to wag. The village was a small place.

'I've been away on business, Chris. I've just got back. Sam and Kyle were not home when I arrived, and I'm trying to find them. That's all.'

'Were you expecting them to be there?'

'Well . . .'

'They'll be off doing something, somewhere. You know what Sam's like. Maybe gone into town to see a movie or visit McDonald's. Gone to the supermarket even?'

'Yes, I'm sure you're right,' he said slowly. 'I just thought I would try one or two obvious places. Thanks for your help.'

'No problem. I'm sure they'll be back soon. Don't worry.'

But that was it: he was worried. He couldn't help it. Sam would have said, if she had planned to do something with Kyle. But she hadn't. She had been looking forward to him coming home. She had said they both were. And he had believed her.

Besides, there were still the old rules. She wouldn't have forgotten them, surely? Never. They were deeply implanted in both their brains. Even if the need for such an agreement had long since passed, they both would always remember never to give the other reason to worry about an unexpected absence or failure to turn up. That golden rule was second nature to them.

But there was no message anywhere. What did it mean?

After a few more phone calls, he grew even more worried. By 7.30 p.m. he had run out of places and people to call. No one, it seemed, had seen anything of either Sam or Kyle after school had finished that afternoon. Most of the people he called were not even sure if they had even seen Sam and Kyle leave the school together.

He made another cup of coffee and considered his options as calmly as he could. The obvious one now was to call the police and say his family were missing, but he was reluctant to do that. It was a big step to take. Doing so might convert a small problem into a big one. It would also mean making the absence of his wife and son a public matter. He wasn't sure he was ready for it to go that far, not yet at least.

But he could think of nothing else he could do, and he did want to do something very badly indeed. As the evening wore on, his concern and anxiety steadily increased. He was becoming afraid something bad, really bad, had happened to his family.

CHAPTER THREE

He phoned the local police station. As he had half-expected, his call was transferred to the main police station in the nearest town, and then to somewhere even more distant. Nighttime service, he assumed. The person he eventually spoke to, more an auxiliary receptionist than a police officer, wasn't much help.

'Unfortunately, the community officer who covers your village is not on duty right now. But we'll forward a message to him, and he'll get back to you as soon as he comes back on duty.'

'When will that be?'

'First thing in the morning.'

'Tomorrow?' he said with exasperation. 'That's no good. This is urgent!'

Already it seemed like a lost cause. If he couldn't speak to a local police officer now, this evening, what was the point?

'What, exactly, is the problem, sir?'

'My wife and son are missing. I returned home this afternoon from a business trip to find them missing. I'm worried about them.'

More detail was requested, and given. His name, his full name. Address. Postcode. Phone number. The minutes ticked away. He grew increasingly frustrated. For God's sake! Were they going to help or not?

'I understand your concern, sir. Unfortunately, there isn't anything we can do at the moment. May I suggest you wait until you can talk it over with the local officer in the morning?'

'You don't understand. Obviously I'm not making myself clear. I'm seriously worried about my wife and son. And it can't wait until tomorrow!'

'The problem, sir, is that we don't regard someone as missing — officially, that is — for twenty-four hours. Until then, we can't launch a missing person inquiry.'

'By then, it might be too late!' he said with despair.

'Your wife could simply be visiting someone, or perhaps her car has broken down? There are all sorts of reasons for her not to be at home just now, don't you think?'

'No, I don't. Her car is still in the garage. I've visited and phoned everywhere and everyone I can think of, and no one seems to know where they are.'

'Perhaps they've just gone for a walk?'

'In this weather? Just as it was getting dark? Without going home from school with our son first, to dress him properly? I really don't think so. Besides, it's nearly nine o'clock now, and it's been dark for several hours.'

'Well, I'll see that the local community officer gives you a call just as soon as I can reach him. I'm sure it will all be sorted out soon.'

And that was that.

What was abundantly clear to him afterwards was that he hadn't been believed. If Kyle had been alone, it would probably have been a different story. The police would have been out in numbers already for a missing child. But given that he was with his mother, they were inclined to put another interpretation on the situation, and to wait and see.

He could almost see their point of view. Either mother and child had gone out somewhere, and been delayed . . . . Either that or the mother, the wife, had decided she had had enough and departed for pastures new. Run away with her fancy man, perhaps, or left home for some other reason best known to herself. Perhaps the husband was a violent man? It was possible, and common enough. That was how the police seemed to be looking at it — as a domestic matter. For twenty-four hours, at least.

Well, so it was a domestic matter, but not in the sense the police were inclined to think at this stage. Something was wrong, terribly wrong. He knew that, felt it deep in his bones. Something bad had happened. His growing fear was that it had nothing to do with his village or the people who were in his life now.

He did wonder if they might have gone for a walk, despite what he'd said on the phone. But when he checked the cupboard under the stairs, and saw that the family's walking boots were all in place, he ruled that out. Sam wouldn't have taken Kyle walking on the moor, or along by the river, in this cold, wet weather anyway, and certainly not without putting on boots and wet weather clothing. She knew only too well how hazardous it could be on the hills in bad weather without the proper gear.

Next, he looked in the garage again, just in case his eyes had deceived him the first time. They had not. Sam's little car was still there. He checked inside it but saw nothing out of the ordinary. Apart from a pair of old sunglasses, there was nothing at all in the car itself. The boot was half-full of the usual stuff: an old coat, several shopping bags needed for trips to the supermarket, spare wheel and associated tools. Nothing extra at all. Sam kept the car as tidy as their home.

After that he ranged around the house, desperate to find something out of the ordinary, something that might provide a clue as to where his family had gone. He found nothing, nothing at all that helped.

He returned to the living room and sat on the sofa, keeping his phone next to him. He willed himself to be still and stared resolutely at the wall opposite, ignoring the painting of the hills that he liked so much, focusing on the blank, white space beside it instead. He conjured up images of his wife and son, and willed them to appear in person before him. There was nothing else he could do. For the moment, at least, he seemed to have exhausted all other possibilities.

Then the phone rang, and the situation suddenly became much worse.

'You know who we are,' a voice said, 'and what we want.'

And he did. He believed he did.

CHAPTER FOUR

Slovakia, 23 April 2004

The place was a dump. One look was enough to see that. But he didn't care. He was across the border, Uzghorod behind him, and he had to stop somewhere. He'd come far enough for one day. It was dark now and he was utterly exhausted.

He got out of the car, taking a small bag containing a dictionary and a few other personal items with him. The bag was all he had, and he was lucky to have that. A few hours ago he would gladly have settled for less, just to get out of Lviv.

He straightened up, stretched his aching back muscles and stood for a few moments, looking around pensively. The forest, dark and brooding, closed right up to the car park. There were a few desultory lights on poles, and a few more in windows in the building behind him, but the place was pretty well deserted. The ski season was over now and the snow just about gone, apart from a few dirty piles in corners the sun didn't reach. Still cold, though. He ducked his head against a sudden gust of icy wind and headed for the entrance.

There was no one in the foyer. The place wasn't big enough to justify a permanently manned reception desk, especially at this time of year. A handwritten notice suggested ringing the hand bell placed nearby on a small wooden table for attention. He glanced around first.

The building was exactly what it had seemed: a small ski chalet. Probably with about a dozen guest rooms. At this time of year it was shabby and looking worn out. It would no doubt be fixed up a bit over the coming summer months, but then a new horde of impoverished youngsters would arrive to trample the industrial carpet, scuff the walls and break the chairs all over again. In season it would be cheap and cheerful, buzzing with the energy and the noise of the young. Right now, it was dead and miserable, and ought to be even cheaper. It suited him perfectly.

He picked up the bell and rang for attention.

A young man who might have been a student, and who was almost certainly very adept on skis, came eventually to see what he wanted.

Speaking in Czech, he said he wanted a room for the night.

'Just for one night?' the man responded in Slovak, which was not so very different a language.

He nodded.

'Two hundred *Slovenských Korún*,' the young man said.

Slovak crowns. Four quid, approximately.

'Fine. Euros OK?'

'Euros, yes. Or dollars.'

He handed over a ten-euro banknote, the only money he had with him. The mayhem back in Lviv had seen to that.

'You will accept *Korún* as change?' the young man asked as he made a calculation with pen and paper.

He nodded and pocketed the change when it came without checking it.

'There is no one else here,' the young man confided. 'So you can choose a room for yourself. The keys are over there,' he added, nodding towards a panel on the wall, home to clusters of keys. 'Help yourself.'

'*Děkuju*. Thank you. Will there be breakfast?'

'Possibly,' the young man said with a sigh. 'If I can find something, I will put it on the table over there for you. And hot water in a thermos jug, for tea or coffee.'

He nodded his thanks and turned away to look for a room, thinking, thank God it's cheap!

On the first floor there was a long corridor, with three or four rooms off to each side. He opened a couple of doors, to see that the rooms were pretty much identical. They were simply furnished, with IKEA-style furniture. Bed, wardrobe, bedside table, all in cheap blond veneer, and a padded chair with a tubular metal frame that might once have been comfortable. There was nothing to choose between the rooms.

The door to one room was partially open. He pushed it open wider, and hastily apologized to the man sitting there in a chair before he pulled back. The man didn't reply.

After that, he decided he didn't need to try any more rooms. They were all the same anyway. So he opened the next door, tossed his bag onto the bed and went back downstairs to get the key.

Sleep didn't come easily. He was tired enough, God knew. But that didn't help. He was on edge, too much running through his mind. He couldn't believe how sudden and catastrophic the end had been in Lviv. Viktor Sirko's wide-ranging empire had turned out to be built on sand, and powerless to resist the incoming tide from the east. Once Yugov and the Russians arrived, it had all gone in a matter of an hour or two — even Viktor himself. Bodies everywhere. Security had been no match for what hit them without warning.

It was a miracle that he had got out in time, and it took some believing that he had. He couldn't have done it without Vlasta's warning. He wouldn't have had a chance.

Leave, she had said when she phoned him. *Go! Just drop everything and leave right now. John, you must — now!*

He grimaced as he recalled how close he had been to laughing at her. The warning had made no sense, had seemed like a practical joke, but somehow she had impressed him enough to humour her. He had followed her instruction and left the main building to walk across the road to the little park, where he was supposed to meet her.

Vlasta did not appear. He still didn't know what had happened to her. From the park he had seen Sirko's enemies arrive in trucks. Perhaps two dozen men. They had stormed the building with automatic weapons and for an agonizing time, there had been sustained gunfire. When it stopped, Viktor was dead, and his businesses in the east taken over. A lot of other people were dead, too.

But he had been lucky, thanks to Vlasta. He had walked away and got out of town, with nothing but the clothes in which he stood. He knew who the attackers were, but there had been nothing he could have done to stop them. There was nothing he could do now either, except hope to survive. He just had to hope that Vlasta had somehow managed it, too.

For several hours he lay awake in this peaceful place in another country, listening to the sound of the building journeying through the night. Heating pipes clanked as they cooled. Floorboards creaked. A sudden gusty wind tugged at the corners of the window for a few minutes. Once he heard voices in the distance, in the depths of the building perhaps, and wondered why the young man who had responded to the bell had said no one else was here. Had he forgotten the guest in the room along the corridor?

Eventually, mercifully, he slept for a while. It was very dark when he awoke. The external lights in the car park had been switched off, and the only light in the room came from his wrist watch on the bedside table. He lay still, listening intently, on edge, automatically ready for flight. But the building was silent now, sleeping at last. There was no noise from outside, either. The wind had dropped, and the world seemed peaceful and still, deceptively so.

But he, at least, was fully awake now. Not rested and recovered. It would take more than a few hours out of the cauldron for that. But he knew he wouldn't sleep again this night.

There was no point lying in bed any longer. The road beckoned. He should be on it, moving, going somewhere — anywhere. Every mile he put behind him would be a mile more distant from the danger zone, if not actually a mile closer to safety.

His watch said it was just after five. If he got up now, he could be on his way by half past. Sooner, perhaps. He got up.

As he dressed, he thought it unlikely that food had been put out yet, even if the young man downstairs had found anything. It didn't matter. He could do without breakfast. He wasn't hungry. Food would probably make him sick anyway, the way he felt.

After a quick wash, he checked the contents of his wallet and winced. Nothing had changed since he gave the man in reception his last banknote. If he ate today, he wouldn't be eating tomorrow. It was as simple and as bad as that. With a shrug, he put the wallet away carefully in a zipped pocket where he kept his passport. That was with him at all times, and always had been these past several years.

He was ready. A last look around the room. Then he left, quietly closing the door after him. The corridor was bathed in dim light from the emergency lighting system. As he headed for the stairs, he passed the other room that had an occupant. The door was open still, and he caught a glimpse of the man sitting in the chair. Another insomniac, he thought with a rueful smile.

He had reached the staircase, and was about to head down it, when he stopped and frowned. Uneasily, he thought that wasn't right. The man. Sitting there, like that. Still?

It was no time for just thinking and wondering. The road was beckoning and he was ready to go. He turned and walked back along the corridor to the room with the open door. The man was still there. He hadn't moved. Even now, with a stranger staring at him from the open doorway, he didn't move a muscle.

He stared for a moment. Then he entered the room and walked over to the man in the chair, sure now that his fellow guest would not move again — ever.

CHAPTER FIVE

There was no pulse. The man was stone cold dead. Shot. Not suicide, either. Murdered.

Not much blood, and not a lot of damage to look at, but you could see where the bullet had entered the skull. A small calibre weapon, and the shooter had been very close when he, or she, had pulled the trigger.

He grimaced and stepped back, his mind racing. What to do? Report it, and get sucked into a police investigation?

He didn't think so. It was time he was away from here. The border, and any pursuit that might be coming, was too close. He didn't suppose for one moment that that had all stopped in Lviv. He couldn't afford to think like that. All Viktor's people, himself included, were at risk.

Still, that aside, what the fuck had gone on here? What was this about?

He thought for a moment. Was it connected to what had happened back there? It couldn't be, surely? But it might be. He couldn't afford to dismiss the possibility. Maybe they had come for him, and got the wrong man? Unlikely, but possible.

He studied the dead man. Late thirties or early forties. Well-built. Probably not particularly tall. Thinning hair. The pale complexion suggested he wasn't a ski enthusiast, or an outdoors guy of any description. Dressed in a good quality brown tweed suit, and collar and tie, he looked more like some young person's visiting businessman father — the young man's downstairs, perhaps? Or a travelling salesman for a prestigious company. Or an academic on holiday, or . . . or anything at all, really. An ordinary sort of guy. But modestly well-off.

There seemed to be nothing to connect him with what had gone down in Ukraine, apart from his having been shot dead so close to the border. He considered a moment longer. Then he stooped to pat the man's jacket. There was something heavy in the breast pocket. He hesitated only briefly before reaching into the pocket to draw out a bulging wallet. It contained a lot of money, in various currencies: dollars, euros, both Czech and Slovak crowns, and even sterling. Some big denomination notes, too.

The breast pocket on the other side of the jacket held a Czech passport — and an American passport. Dual nationality? He frowned and studied the passports thoughtfully. They carried the same photo, but they had been issued in different names. Which was the genuine one, he wondered? Either of them?

The photo was a bit of a shock. He couldn't take his eyes off it for a moment. The cogs of his mind began to whir ever faster. Then he shook his head, putting the discovery to one side for the moment.

The man's right hand was out of sight, tucked under a loose cushion. He leant down and gently eased up the cushion. The hand had firm hold of a gun, a Glock 17 pistol. That was another surprise.

He stared at the gun for a moment, thinking that the guy must have had some warning, or premonition, but simply hadn't been able to get it out fast enough. Why the hell had he stuck it under a cushion but kept hold of it? What did that mean?

He shrugged. Then he worked the fingers loose and took the gun away. He placed it, together with the wallet and passports, on the bedside table. Next, he turned his attention to the man's travel bag resting on the bed. He zipped the bag open and stared with incredulity at the contents. Jesus Christ!

By then, he had expected to find money — but not this much.

He sat heavily on the bed and studied the neat bundles of banknotes inside the unassuming green holdall. He couldn't even begin to guess how much there was. But it was a vast amount.

He took out a few of the bundles, and confirmed that the bundles underneath were just as real as the ones on top. Mostly dollars, as well. An absolute bloody fortune!

Reaching to the bottom, he felt beneath the loose panel that served to stiffen the bag and pulled out two more passports. One was German, the other French. He reached down again and pulled out a Russian passport.

Like the first two passports he had seen, they carried different names but the same photograph. He stared at the photograph in the Russian passport. He couldn't help it. The photograph looked uncannily like the picture he saw every morning in the bathroom mirror.

Shit! What to do? He thought for a moment. Just a moment. No more. Then he shook his head and put everything back in the bag.

Belatedly, he stood up and crossed the room to close the door. He knew exactly what he was going to do. He had been given a get-out-of-jail-free card, and he was going to use it.

For the next five minutes he worked quickly and methodically, going through every drawer and cupboard in the room, and every pocket in every garment he could find. He searched for paperwork and for anything else that might prove useful or informative.

Every instinct but one told him to get out — to get out now! He hadn't the time for this shit.

But the instinct that was the one exception told him he did have a little time, a brief moment, and he had to hang on and do things right. There would be no coming back, no second chance. That was the instinct, the voice he listened to. It was the voice of logic.

Before he left the room, he placed the car keys and the passport he had arrived with on the bedside table. Then he thought better of it and picked the passport up to slip back into his pocket. He didn't think he would be needing it again. He was Jack Olsson now. But you never knew.

CHAPTER SIX

He let himself out of the front door and stood for a moment at the top of the steps leading to the entrance while he surveyed the car park in the grey half-light of the pre-dawn. Although he had been told there were no other guests, there were a dozen cars parked outside. Some, surrounded by heaps of frozen snow, looked as if they had been there all winter.

Which one was it? He pressed the button on the key and was rewarded by the sight of an Audi lighting up. It was nearby, in a cleared space. He didn't need to dig it out.

He set off across the gravelled forecourt, and was immediately assailed by searing cold and a whiff of rotting snow and old diesel fumes. It was a grim, icy morning, spring not yet able to make a firm claim on the land. There was no one in sight and he doubted if any vehicle had entered or left the car park that morning. People would be stirring, somewhere, but they were not outside yet. Even the village dogs were still tucked up in their kennels. It was a good time to be leaving.

A quick walk round the Audi assured him that the tyres were sound. He got in and started the engine first go. Switched on the heater and fan, and directed the air flow at the windscreen. The glass fogged instantly. He wiped it clear with one hand. Then he switched on the lights and backed out of the parking bay. Time he was gone.

He was on edge. One of the many thoughts troubling him, an insidious little thing nagging away at the back of his mind, was that whoever had killed Olsson — or whatever his name really was — had walked away from a huge pile of money. Why? Even if the man himself had been the target, why ignore such a fortune? Who would do that, and why?

He could suggest an answer, but he didn't like it. The murder could have been a targeted killing, with the killer operating under instruction. Taking a pile of money from the victim was not part of the job, and the killer had not dared to risk it. He had feared the consequences. So whoever had ordered the hit was not someone to be taken lightly.

He paused and sat with the car in neutral for a moment, drumming his fingers on the steering wheel while he worked it out. It didn't take him long. It meant someone else would probably be along shortly to check and investigate, and perhaps to lay claim to what Olsson had been carrying. At first light, perhaps. Any minute now even.

Fuck it! He'd take his chances.

In other circumstances, he might have enjoyed the early morning drive. Now he just wanted to get moving and put some distance behind him. But he still drove carefully. There was ice on the road, and no sign of a recent gritting. He couldn't afford to be immobilized in a ditch. Especially not now, he thought with a wince. How would he explain the money?

The money. The money was a worry, as well as an opportunity. For the moment, it had even eclipsed thoughts of the debacle in Lviv. A big worry. But he was still keeping it. Damn right he was! He had to have something for the time he'd put in out here.

His headlights lit up the tunnel through the forest. Tall, dark conifers on each side. The edges of the road were demarcated by linear mounds of dirty snow pushed aside and left by the ploughs over many months. A small herd of deer crossed the road a little way ahead, bounding and leaping to escape his lights. He dipped the beams and slowed, as much for his own sake as for theirs. Deer were big and heavy enough to do significant damage to a car designed for high-speed motoring on the autobahn.

Twenty minutes later he began to relax a little. He even grinned. Hell, he'd done it!

For the time being, he cautioned himself. But now he would have Olsson's killers on his back, as well as anyone coming after him from Lviv, or from further east.

The cops as well, probably, when the people running the ski chalet discovered the body and raised the alarm. But what could they tell the police about him? He hadn't even been asked to sign a guest book. So they didn't have so much as a forged name for him. Just a description from the young guy on reception, if he could remember anything at all about the departed guest.

There would be something about the cars. Maybe the owner or manager would remember that their first guest had arrived in an Audi, not a Skoda. Maybe. But perhaps not if the only person around had been the young guy who had let him in last night.

What about the Skoda left in the car park? He thought for a moment and shook his head. It wasn't his. He'd just taken it off the street. There was nothing to connect it with him.

Had he left anything inside the car? He didn't think so. He'd had virtually nothing with him. Just the one little bag. Nothing else? Just fingerprints. That could be a problem.

He grimaced and then thought, oh, to hell with it! What was done was done. There was no going back.

To improve his chances, he decided to leave the road for Kosice that went on eventually to Bratislava, on the western edge of Slovakia. Instead, he opted to head south into Hungary. Putting another international border behind him might help, might give him crucial time while officialdom sorted out questions of jurisdiction, if they were on his trail.

Once in Hungary, he would head down to Vienna and then west to Salzburg, and on into Germany. With luck, he would be moving fast enough to get across a few borders before anybody looking for him had any idea where he was. The Schengen Agreement meant that borders in the EU were not what they used to be, but it didn't mean that police forces could still operate only on their own patch. Not every country had signed up to it anyway.

Things were looking up, he decided with some satisfaction. He was well out of the hell hole that was Ukraine, and soon he would be deep into the safe part of Europe. And he had money. Lots of it! He chuckled at the thought. He could do a hell of a lot with the money. Even pay for petrol.

He kept going all day, and as it was getting dark, took a room in a pension not far from Regensburg in Bavaria. It was another ski chalet, basically, but several classes better than the previous one he'd stayed in. It looked lived in but well looked after, and not the kind of place where you might stumble across dead bodies nobody else had noticed.

He could have kept going, but he stopped when he did because he needed to work out what he was going to do next. Now he was out of the immediate danger zone, there was no point continuing to run like a headless chicken. He needed to run more like a wounded fox, a damaged creature admittedly, but one with all its wits about it still.

And there was Vlasta to think of. What on earth had become of her?

Taking stock, there was a lot of paper to wade though and assimilate. There was almost no unnecessary personal information amongst it, but it seemed that the man — Jack Olsson, according to the American passport — had been an arms salesman. He had been looking to sell a range of weapons, probably to anyone who expressed an interest and had the money to pay for them.

It looked as though he had been probing markets in Ukraine and Romania, and possibly Moldova. Not Transnistria, though, that slender strip of land between

Moldova and Ukraine. Russians, and Russian weapons, if not Russia itself, had control there.

Probably not Slovakia either, where Olsson had met his end. The capital, Bratislava, on the other side of the country, was where he would have been if he had wanted to sell to the Slovaks. No, on balance, he had probably been focusing on Ukraine, given all the pressure the country had been getting from Russia in the east. The Ukrainians needed more and better weapons from somewhere. Otherwise, they could forget about the idea of being independent.

What about the money, all those American dollars? There was not much doubt about what that was for. It certainly wasn't money that Olsson had been paid. Salesmen didn't come away with bags of money that could be taken back from them once they left the building and turned the corner. It would have been intended to smooth the wheels of commerce.

In Ukraine, and everywhere else in eastern Europe, cash to smooth negotiations was an essential tool of the trade, just as it was when western countries went on sales drives to Saudi Arabia, or anywhere in Africa and the Indian sub-continent. Anywhere in the world, if the truth be known. Even America. Maybe especially America.

Well, he concluded, he would put it to a damned sight better use than Olsson would have done. He was sure of that. No one would be killed by it, now it was in his hands.

He wondered about Olsson. Who was he? Where had he come from? Who did he represent? A government, a company? There were so many passports in his possession that it was hard to know which, if any, was proof of nationality or citizenship.

A citizen of the world, then? He smiled grimly. Probably not. Somebody, somewhere, would have claim on him — and on the money. Whether it was a country or a company was a moot point, and scarcely seemed to matter anyway. Olsson had lost out. The money was his now.

This extraordinary windfall had arrived at exactly the right time. He had needed money badly. What he had earned with Viktor over the past couple of years had all been lost when he scrambled to get out of Lviv. He had nothing to show for his time there, nothing at all.

No matter. He was alive, and now he had financial compensation for what he had lost. It was a fair trade. He should have been as dead as the rest of them, and would have been if it hadn't been for Vlasta. He certainly couldn't complain now.

He stood up and wandered around the room. Was he safe here? He doubted it. Safe for the moment, perhaps, but the people who had stormed Lviv would know of him. They would be coming. He needed to make plans, and fast. Another opportunity to re-establish himself would not come his way. This was it. He had to make good use of it. Viktor, bless his soul, would have expected nothing less of him.

As for Vlasta, well, all he could do for the moment was hope she was safe. He had to put all thoughts of her to one side until he was safe. She, too, would have expected nothing less of him.

CHAPTER SEVEN

Washington DC, 3 September 2014

George Riley took his time getting there. He was in no hurry, and the crowds on the streets of the capital were something of a novelty to him these days. He was a stranger here now, he mused with a wry smile, and glad to be so.

Rafferty's had received a lick of fresh paint since he was last here. Still a bar, though. He paused before he went inside and ran his eyes over the once familiar exterior. Still a bar, and no doubt still a good and quiet place to meet after a long, hard day.

He smiled and headed for the entrance. He didn't miss those days, not really. He'd had his time here, in this city, and he wasn't sorry it was over. He would just have liked to have been twenty or thirty years younger.

Ted Pearson was waiting for him at a quiet table towards the rear of the room. He had a beer in front of him and now he signalled to a waiter that he wanted one for the new arrival.

'George! Good to see you. How the heck are you?'

'Just fine, Ted, thanks. You? It's been a while, hasn't it?'

Pearson was on his feet by then, and they shook hands.

'Retirement's suiting you, eh? I can see that from the look on your face.'

Riley chuckled. He was happy to chew the fat with an old colleague, one he almost counted a friend; they went back so far.

'Country living suits me just fine, Ted. It's a bit stressful at times, but no worse than here — and it's no use complaining anyway.'

'Stressful? What — wondering how deep the snow's gonna be? Calculating if you've chopped enough wood to last the winter?'

'All of that!' Riley grinned. 'How about you, Ted? Things good with you?'

'Oh, you know. Nothing changes here. It's still just one damned thing after another.'

Riley could imagine. He thought Ted looked as if he needed some retirement himself. His face was older, five or six years older, and what was left of his hair was Brillo-pad grey now, going on white. The paunch that had always been there was significantly bigger, too.

'To tell the truth, George,' Pearson confided, 'another couple of years will be enough for me — if I last that long.'

'Making plans, eh?'

'I sure am. But I'll be going back West. Vermont wouldn't suit me as well as it obviously does you.'

'I can't complain,' Riley admitted.

'I got a few little things to settle, and then I'm out of here.'

He paused and squinted into the distance. Riley waited, and sipped his beer. Something was coming. He knew that. He'd known it ever since he took the phone call. He just didn't have a clue what it was.

'Ted?' he prompted.

'Sorry, George. I was miles away, thinking of days gone by.'

'That can be a bad sign, old friend. And you shouldn't let anyone know, in case they start talking. Next thing you know, there'll be a shrink waiting to interview you.'

Pearson grinned and picked up his glass of beer. 'Remember Jack Olsson?' he asked quietly before taking a long swallow.

Riley wondered if he was hallucinating. Alternatively, the acoustics in Rafferty's were so strange he was picking up some weird stuff. Just noise, basically. Random noise that didn't make any sense at all. That must be what it was, all it was. But Ted was looking at him, staring at him, waiting for him to say something meaningful.

He shook his head. 'My hearing,' he muttered ruefully. 'Maybe it's tinnitus. I ought to get it checked out. I blame the chain saw. You don't always bother to put on the ear muffs when you're in a hurry. You just want to have at it, and get the job done.'

'George! Answer the question, dammit, not that I really need you to.'

Riley shut up and stared at his beer for a moment. 'Jack Olsson?' he repeated slowly. 'Did I really hear you say that name?'

'Remember him, George? Of course you do.'

Riley knew now why he had been asked here today. It wasn't old friendship, after all. It was business, old business.

'What's this about, Ted? Something come up?'

'We never did know what happened to him, did we?'

Riley shook his head. It was true. Jack, a good buddy, had simply disappeared one time. He had gone to Ukraine, and never been heard of again. His best buddy. Disappeared. Life seemed like shit sometimes.

'How long ago was it?' Pearson asked reflectively.

'A few years.'

'Ten, near enough.'

They sat quietly for a moment, resurrecting memories.

'He was a good man,' Riley said softly.

'One of the best.'

'So what's this about, Ted?'

The mood suddenly changed.

Pearson locked eyes with him and said, 'We think we may have discovered what happened to him. We want you to go over there, to Europe, and confirm it.'

'I'm retired, Ted.'

'You're still the best man for the job.'

For Jack Olsson's sake, Riley heard Pearson out.

'As you know, George, we didn't have a clue what had happened to old Jack. He simply disappeared off our radar. At the time, we assumed he got caught up in the attack in Lviv that wiped out Viktor Sirko. Remember him?'

'Vaguely. Jack was visiting him, wasn't he?' Riley paused and frowned. 'Doing some business there, I seem to recall.'

Pearson nodded. 'That's right. We were channelling arms through Sirko because we didn't think the West's guarantees to Ukraine were worth a damn. Hell, we expected the President to look the other way when — not if — the shit hit the fan. But all was supposed to be sweetness and light in those early Putin days. The Oval Office didn't want to hear a word against him.'

'And they didn't.'

'When push came to shove, the guarantees made to Ukraine by the US, Great Britain and the Kremlin weren't worth the paper they were written on. Some of us knew that all along.'

'What about Jack?' Riley pressed.

'Yeah. Poor old Jack. Just recently a few things have come together that tell us how he ended up.'

'He's not alive?'

Pearson shook his head. 'Sadly. We're sure of that, if nothing else. Just recently, the Slovaks forwarded DNA material from some guy they'd had in their morgue for ten years. Don't ask me why now! But they did it. A new broom doing some house cleaning, probably. Wanting to get the guy buried, or otherwise out of the way.'

'Maybe they're wanting more friendship? Afraid it'll be their turn next, when Putin gets finished with Ukraine.'

'Yeah.' Pearson shook his head. 'We really don't need this, do we?'

It wasn't a question that demanded an answer.

'Anyway,' Pearson continued, 'to cut a long story short, we identified the body as Jack Olsson.'

'In Slovakia?'

Pearson nodded.

'And they really didn't know who and what he was all this time?'

'Apparently. He was just a body to them. All his documentation was gone, along with a pile of money. His car, too. All they had was a body, and a car that wasn't Jack's. They could make nothing of it.'

'You mentioned money. How much?'

'Ten million bucks.'

'Cash?'

'Yeah.'

Riley whistled.

'Anyway, it was Jack Olsson. So now we know Jack died in a small hotel in eastern Slovakia.'

Riley thought that was quite likely. The easy thing for Jack to have done would have been to board a plane in Kiev, but that could be risky if you were carrying stuff that would be hard to explain. Like $10,000,000. Safer to slip over the border at some quiet, out of the way, crossing point. Normally, at least. Perhaps he had been followed on this occasion.

'So either he hadn't been able to get to Sirko with the money or the deal fell through. Either way, he was on his way back out.'

'Something like that. We don't really know. But Sirko was hit at that time, remember? So maybe Jack aborted his mission.'

Riley recalled all that. It was starting to come back to him now, all this stuff he had put into deep storage these past few years.

'Did the Slovaks say how Jack died?'

'He was shot. Bullet in the head.'

Riley grimaced.

'He was staying in some ski village, some little hotel there. A pension, I think they call it. The season was over. But it was still cold. Nothing happening.

'The hotel had only one other guest at the time. Their record keeping wasn't up to much. So we don't know who that guest was — not from the hotel register, at least.

'By the time the cops were brought in, the other guy had disappeared. They had no idea who he was. But they searched his room and the car he had left behind, and collected the evidence, what there was of it.'

'What did they get?'

'DNA's wonderful stuff, isn't it?' Pearson said, looking up with a wry smile. 'They got it for both the dead guy — Jack — and the other guest, the guy who might have killed him. So they had it, but they didn't do anything with it for ten years. Then they sent it all stateside.'

Riley nodded thoughtfully and mulled it over. 'Another beer?' he asked eventually.

'You buying?'

'Sure. My pension will stand a couple of beers.' He waved the waiter over and ordered, giving himself more time to think. 'That all you got?' he asked when he turned back to Pearson. 'A pile of DNA?'

'Pretty much. At least, until recently it was.'

Taking delivery of the beers took a couple of minutes. Then they got right back at it, the pace quickening as George Riley found himself being expertly reeled in.

'You familiar with the automatic DNA matching programme we run?' Pearson asked.

'Not really. I've heard rumours of it, but I know nothing about it.'

'It's big stuff. We do a lot of it now, mostly terrorism related.'

'Like the matching of voice recordings?'

'Yeah. That's it. Exactly. Anyway, we do it for recorded crime scenes. Just automatically punch the data in, and see if anything matches up.'

'So what have you got?'

'It's very interesting. Some guy in England had his house burgled a little while ago — and guess what?'

'You're kidding?' Riley stared, and thought about it for a moment. Then he smiled and shook his head. 'I don't believe it!'

Pearson grinned. 'You'd better! It's the same guy who ten years ago spent a night in the same little old ski lodge in Slovakia where Jack Olsson was staying and got himself murdered.'

'A Brit?'

Pearson nodded. 'Seems to be. We'd like you to go over there and take a look at the guy, George. Figure out if he really is the one who shot Jack. And if he is,' he added ominously, 'do something about it.'

CHAPTER EIGHT

London, 26 April 2004

He debated dumping the car in France and continuing on foot, or hitching a lift. He didn't do it. After a couple of days, the car felt like home. He liked it. It held him and his belongings, such as they were. Not least, it held the bag with the money. How could he cope without it?

Yet he knew the car would have to be abandoned at some point. It was a hire vehicle, belonging to one of the big car hire firms. It could be traced, and might even have a tracker fitted. He didn't want a search ending up at his door.

Wherever he abandoned it, the car would be an arrow pointing to where he was going next. But in that sense, he supposed, it didn't really matter whether he abandoned it now or when he was across the Channel. Anyone who knew of him would also know he was English. It would be obvious where he'd gone. So he might as well keep it for now, and dump it on the other side.

In Victoria he parked on a side street, picked up the money bag and walked away from the Audi. He took a cab to King's Cross. Then he took another one to Euston, and one after that to Paddington. Finally, he took the tube and surface line north and west to Hatch End, where he booked into a nondescript B & B. His movements were random. Following in his footsteps, or retracing them, would be a tough challenge for anyone who wasn't close behind right now.

Even then, he didn't stand still. Before night arrived, he bought an old banger from a nearby garage that offered good deals, paying cash for it. What he got was a fifteen-year-old Volkswagen Golf that set him back £500, a price he thought he could risk paying with banknotes without raising eyebrows. Already, he was beginning to lament the lack of plastic he could use safely, but he was determined not to leave a trail. That had to be a priority.

Once he had the car — a gift for his seventeen-year-old son, he said — he toured a couple of neighbourhood shopping centres, where he bought clothes and a few other necessities. His purchases did little to reduce the cash mountain in the bag.

There followed an uneasy night, one full of foreboding and tension. He believed he was in the clear, but he couldn't be sure. A little voice kept whispering in his ear, reminding him that it wasn't necessarily so. In the morning he quit the guest house very early and headed north, heading for a place where he hoped to feel more secure and comfortable. The supposed anonymity of the big city didn't work for him.

North Northumberland, the English Borders, was where he was headed. Not exactly home — he'd never really had one of those — but it was somewhere of which he had fond childhood memories. It was where one of his grandmothers had lived all her life, and where his own mother had spent her growing up years. He had himself spent a couple of summers there, glorious times in his memory, and it was where he wanted to be right now. He had to take stock and build a new life for himself, and he could think of nowhere better to do it.

On the way, he traded for a better car. He got half of what he'd paid for the Golf, and put in that and another £500 in cash to buy a Golf a year or two younger and in slightly better condition. Again, he restrained himself. It wouldn't do to splash the cash too obviously. He didn't want to be remembered. He just wanted wheels that would serve their purpose for a little while longer.

At an outdoor supplier's near Bawtry he bought a tent, a sleeping bag and a few other eminently practical items. For his son, he explained, who was going on a school camping trip. The salesman nodded and recommended taking a couple of maps, as well. He chose maps of North Wales, Snowdonia, where he said his son was going.

Food, he thought when he left the shop. That's what I need next. A Tesco superstore not far away provided him with enough groceries to fill the boot of the car. He also bought a little gas camping stove there, and some cooking utensils. And a couple of large water bottles. They were all from an aisle they were getting ready for the summer season.

Back on the road, he felt satisfied. He was self-sufficient now. His new life had begun. He had the time and freedom to think. Most of all, he wanted to think about Vlasta, and what could be done. Was she alive even? He had no idea. All he could do was hope. God, how he missed her!

First, he camped for a few days at a site near Wooler, in the foothills of the Cheviots. Then he moved over to the coast and pitched his tent at Beadnell, all the time watching his back. When he was satisfied, he moved to the Clennell Hall campsite, near Alwinton. There, he was closer to where he wanted to be. Finally, he drove into the village, and looked around the place of which he had such happy memories.

It hadn't changed much. But even here, it seemed, the population was growing. There were a lot of new houses. Yet the ancient parish church was still there, as was the war memorial in the centre of the village. Majestic trees, a mixture of oak, horse chestnut and sycamore, still surrounded the green. There was more traffic than he remembered, but to someone more used to London the centre of the village was almost a pedestrianized zone.

He was satisfied. He could live here, he decided. He just didn't want to do it alone.

For many days he had been phoning Vlasta at intervals, without success. All he had ever got was the standard voice inviting him to leave a message, which he never did. He worried that the phone might be a way of tracing him, but he shrugged it off. He had no choice. Not to use the phone would mean abandoning Vlasta altogether. He had no other means of contacting her, assuming she wasn't dead like her father.

He phoned once more, this time from the village, with the same result. For a moment he was almost overcome by despair. Then he shrugged and got himself back on track. He would find her. If she was alive still, he would find her — or she him.

What gave him hope still, expectations even, was the simple fact that Vlasta had warned him to leave. Surely she would not have remained in the fire zone herself when she knew terrible events were about to unfold there? It was at least possible that she had been some distance away at the time. Otherwise she would surely have tried to help her father, and died with him.

He shied away from the question of how Vlasta could have known something was about to kick off. He didn't want to go there. Not now. Not yet.

Back at the campsite near Alwinton, he took stock and thought some more about what he was going to do, and how he was going to go about it. He would continue trying to reach Vlasta, and continue hoping and believing that she was alive still, but there were also other issues for him now. He couldn't be a permanent holidaymaker, living on campsites, for example. He needed to get on with making a new life for himself.

Although it had been a lifeline tossed to him by a kindly fate, the money was also a worry now. What on earth was he to do with it?

An inventory had told him that he had seven or eight million worth in sterling — depending on the exchange rates — in his possession, mostly in dollars. It was a big responsibility, he thought with a wry smile. It was taking some looking after. He daren't let it out of his sight.

Along the way, he had purchased a rucksack for the money, and dumped the holdall. That had made it easier to carry. But the question of what to do with it remained.

For the moment, he was still carrying the damned rucksack everywhere he went. He daren't risk leaving it in the tent or the car. Soon he needed to get it off his back and into a safe place, and he needed to do that without provoking awkward and dangerous questions.

Then there was the matter of his identity. Who was he? Somehow, now he was back in Northumberland, he no longer felt like Jack Olsson, or even John Carlisle, the name he had used in Ukraine. He felt much more like John Tait, the name he had come into the world with. It wasn't the name he had used for many years but he felt surprisingly comfortable with it. Was there any reason not to revert to it? He couldn't see any.

John Tait had a passport, just as John Carlisle and Jack Olsson did, and Tait wasn't a name anybody searching for him would be looking out for. John Tait also had a bank account, and a safe deposit box where he kept his passport.

Now he was here, he couldn't see any compelling reason to use either the Carlisle or the Olsson identity. He would keep them both, in case of need, but he was going to be John Tait all over again from now on.

That settled, he started looking around for somewhere more permanent to live.

With the money in his rucksack, he could easily have afforded to buy the dozen most expensive houses in the village, but he hadn't yet worked out how he could safely use the money, except in small dollops at a time. He could rent, though, trickling money through his existing bank account for the purpose. So that's what he did.

He found a cottage he liked well enough on the edge of the village and took out the standard six-month lease. The cottage was furnished and available immediately. He sorted things out with the owners, an elderly couple, and moved in the very next day. So now he had an address.

He was self-employed, he told the owners and the bank, and looking to start up a business in the area. That, and the address, gave him apparent legitimacy in the eyes of anyone curious about his circumstances.

Next, he needed to legitimize some transport. There was no paperwork with the Golf, which was pretty well clapped-out anyway. He needed to have a decent car that he owned legally, one that he could tax and insure legitimately.

In Morpeth he visited a dealer and bought another Golf, a much newer one, signing up to make monthly payments that would not raise eyebrows at his bank. He picked up his new car, together with all the paperwork, the next day.

He drove his old Golf into the centre of Newcastle and left it in a long-stay car park in Byker, unlocked and with the keys in the ignition. Then he caught a bus back into the city centre, and another one to Morpeth, where he picked up his new ride and drove back to the valley in it.

That was something else he could cross off his to-do list, he thought with satisfaction. His new life was starting to take shape. Things were coming together nicely.

CHAPTER NINE

Something else he needed to do was work out what he was going to do for a living. It would be better if people could see he had some sort of occupation. Besides, he was going to need something to do for his own peace of mind and sense of self-worth. A life of idleness held no appeal whatsoever. For now, though, all that would have to wait. He had no idea what the answer was, and meanwhile there were more pressing matters to address.

For one, he still had no idea what had happened to Vlasta, and he did desperately need to know.

Then there was the money. It was going to be difficult to use. He knew that. Banks and other recipients of cash were all under legal requirement to report unusual movements of money these days. The movements didn't even have to be big — just unusual. Even casinos, traditionally favoured for laundering money, were no doubt under continuing observation and monitoring by somebody.

The short-term solution was to keep a small amount to meet his immediate needs and store the rest. For storage, he thought he might use a bank's safe deposit box, the traditional answer for people looking to store cash, but virtually all the banks — including his own — had either stopped providing the service or were in the process of closing it down.

That was what he found when he went to use the deposit box he had rented for some years. He was under notice to quit, with the end date not far away. Cost cutting, so often the justification for change, was once again invoked by his unapologetic bank.

A search on his new laptop revealed that a number of companies had stepped into the gap and were offering some kind of storage facility for valuables. The cost varied wildly, not that cost mattered much to him in the circumstances in which he found himself.

More importantly, the companies in question all seemed to be located in either London or the Midlands. They were the areas with the large and prosperous Asian populations that comprised a large part of the market for such a service. Family gold and jewellery, often handed down between the generations, was far too valuable and dangerous to keep at home, seemingly.

He grimaced. He didn't want to store the money so far away. What else could he do? There must be something.

In the end, he went for a small secure storage unit provided by a nationwide company that had a depot in Wallsend, on Tyneside. Mostly, it seemed, they stored stuff for folks who were going to be working abroad for a year or two. Furniture and personal belongings. So he bought a load of second-hand furniture and household goods, and delivered it himself in a van he rented for the purpose. He hid the money bag inside the washing machine.

Security wasn't what it would be in the heart of the jewellery district in Birmingham, perhaps, or in a Swiss bank in London, but it seemed good enough. His cache of old furniture was no more likely to be broken into and stolen than anyone else's in the depot. The risk was worth taking. He'd slept with that damned bag long enough.

The money he needed for now he kept back. He wanted to forget about the rest of it, and think about the things that really mattered to him. He wasn't prepared to serve as a guard for a bag of money for the rest of his life. To hell with that!

Something else he did was study job adverts in local papers and on the web. He had no idea what to look for in particular. Working for himself seemed a good idea in principle, but doing what?

One thing he knew was that he was keeping well away from his old life and work. He'd had enough of working as an adviser with Special Forces in conflict zones. It was too dangerous for him to carry on doing that. His time had run out. He knew enough to quit while he was still ahead.

And all the time, somewhere in his mind, whatever else he was doing, he was thinking of Vlasta. Every day he phoned her on the special phone that held no number but hers. Every time he let the phone ring five times, and then he rang another five times immediately afterwards. Their special code, on the special phones they had each acquired for the purpose.

In their world, their dangerous, if exciting, world, such arrangements had been necessary because they had known that one day they might be needed. That day had come.

But there was never a response. So all he could do was fret, and worry. He began to despair.

He was in the kitchen, taking washing from the tumble dryer, when the phone rang. He listened, automatically counting the rings. Five. Five only.

He stopped what he was doing, dropped everything and ran through to the living room. Just as he reached the phone, it began to ring again. Five times. Five times!

CHAPTER TEN

He snatched the phone up and put it to his ear. He said nothing, waiting, hardly daring to breathe. The silence grew.

'John?'

Thank God! His eyes closed briefly with relief.

'Vlasta! Are you all right? Where are you?'

The words, the sentences, tumbled out of him. He scarcely knew what to ask first.

'I'm OK, John. I'm fine. Safe. You?'

'Me, too. Where are you?'

'Better not to say, perhaps. You know?'

What did that mean? Was there someone with her, listening in, or was she being cautious on principle? He had almost forgotten the rules when it came to safe mobile phone use.

'Of course,' he said. 'You're quite right. But can I take it you're not where I last saw you?'

Lviv, he meant. All those weeks ago. An eternity.

'Not there, no. Somewhere safe for now, I think. And you?'

'I came home.'

'Good. I thought you would. I hoped you would. This is no country for you, especially now.'

He wanted to hear about the disaster, and how deep it ran, but not yet. They hadn't the time.

'Will you join me?' he asked instead, daring to hope.

'Of course. It's what I want to do.'

'Good. Come soon, Vlasta.'

'Very soon, John. There's nothing left here for me either now. They took everything.'

So things were as bad as he had feared. He grimaced. There was nothing left. But his relief that Vlasta was at least safe was immeasurable.

'I gathered that,' he said gently. 'I'm very sorry about Viktor, and the others. But at least we have survived.'

'So far,' she said.

Yes. So far, he thought afterwards.

He would meet her in London. She would fly into Heathrow and make her way to a hotel he knew and would book in Bayswater, where he would meet her. That was all she needed to know, he said. She should leave the rest to him.

She hesitated, and he guessed it was because she would prefer him to meet her at the airport.

'We'll do it this way,' he said gently. 'It's safer.'

'Yes,' she said with a weary sigh, but trusting him. 'We need to be sure.'

She texted him before she left Kiev, and then again when her plane landed at Heathrow. He sighed with relief. She had not been prevented from leaving. She was here at last!

Like so many others waiting outside Arrivals, he held up a strip of cardboard in lieu of a proper message board. The name on it was not hers, nor did it belong to anyone else he knew. But the cardboard justified his presence. He wanted to avoid appearing suspicious to anyone who might be watching out for Vlasta.

He saw her emerge, and for a moment he held his breath, torn between joy at seeing her again and fear for her safety. Even in London she was in peril. Possibly even more so, given the size of the Russian community. Not all Russians in London were peace loving, honest and decent people.

There would be plenty amongst them who would happily take Yugov's shilling.

Vlasta made her way towards a taxi. Just before she reached it, two men came from nowhere to close up behind her. Heavy-set men, wearing leather jackets and jeans, they were moving fast. There could be little doubt about their target.

He moved fast himself, closing in on the three of them in a second or two. Vlasta didn't know what was behind her, but the two men behind her had no idea what was behind them either.

He jumped and stamped on the back of one man's leg, causing him to collapse with a cry. As his partner turned, John pretended to trip and slammed into him with his shoulder, sending him sprawling aside. In the resultant mêlée, he managed to stamp heavily on the first man's hand.

'Sorry!' he said. 'An accident. Here, let me help you.'

But he melted into the crowd without doing anything at all to help, having seen Vlasta getting into a taxi and closing the door after her. It had been so neatly done that no one in the crowd seemed to have noticed anything terribly amiss.

He had pre-booked them both into the hotel. Vlasta was sitting in the lobby, waiting for him, when he arrived. She looked very relieved to see him. He could see in her face the strain she had been under.

He smiled to reassure her and gestured. She picked up the one bag she had with her and joined him to wait for a lift. He took her hand and squeezed gently. She briefly pressed her face into his shoulder in response. They said nothing. He wondered if her heart was beating as fast as his.

With a sharp ping, the doors of the lift began to open. They stepped inside and let the doors close again. Then he took hold of her and hugged her hard, whispering her name. She wrapped her arms around him and looked up, smiling. He kissed her fiercely. Then the lift stopped and a disembodied voice said they were on the third floor.

He took the bag from her and ushered her out into the corridor. There was no one in sight. 'We're not stopping,' he said briskly.

She nodded, and didn't look at all surprised.

He ushered her towards a staircase and they headed back down. At the bottom of the stairs he opened an emergency door and quickly led the way outside, and through a loading bay and a staff car park.

'You didn't notice anybody else?' he asked over his shoulder.

'No. Only the men you dealt with. But it doesn't mean no others were there.'

'True,' he said with a nod.

He glanced around as they left the car park. The narrow access lane was empty. He took her arm and led the way into the main street, both of them walking quickly.

'Two blocks,' he said. 'That's all.'

She nodded.

The Golf was waiting for them in a long-stay car park. He wasted no time getting Vlasta in and setting off. Traffic was heavy but he eased his way through smoothly and began a complicated sequence of manoeuvres intended to confuse anyone who might have been trying to follow them. Only after twenty minutes, when they hit the M25 at last, did he begin to ease off and relax.

'Vlasta,' he said at last, smiling at her. 'Vlasta, darling. You're really here!'

'At last!' she agreed.

She laughed and pushed her head into his shoulder again. He had forgotten how she did that.

'And you're OK?'

'Yes, I think so.' She shrugged. 'It's been difficult at times, but here I am. It's so good to see you again, John. Sometimes I didn't believe it would ever happen.'

'But you kept the faith, and here you are,' he said with a grin. 'Welcome to your new life, sweetheart!'

An hour later, just outside Peterborough, they stopped at a Premier Inn, where he had made a reservation.

'Is it safe?' Vlasta asked, looking around anxiously before they got out of the car.

'I think so,' he assured her. 'I'm sure we weren't followed, and there's no reason for anyone to be watching this place. We'll be OK here. We'll stay the night. Then we'll press on.'

'Where are we going, John?'

'Northwards,' he told her with a grin. 'Just about as far as you can go in England.'

'And what will we do when we get there?'

'I've thought of something,' he said confidently. 'I have an idea. But I don't want to talk about it now. You're too tired.'

It was a little strange at first. They hadn't seen each other for all those months, and in that time so much had happened to them both. They were not exactly strangers, but they were no longer used to each other, either. It was a time to be gentle. There was so much catching up to do, but they did it gently. As Vlasta said, they had the rest of their lives for that.

Let's hope so, he thought, smiling agreement.

CHAPTER ELEVEN

Vlasta was tired, very tired. By the time he got her back to the valley, she was utterly exhausted. He could see that. He didn't need to ask for confirmation.

'Where are we, John?'

'Home,' he said with a smile. 'This is where I thought we might stay, at least for a while.'

'Good.'

He parked and helped her out of the car, and then led her indoors.

'You're falling asleep on your feet,' he said, wrapping his arms around her. 'The best thing for you is bed.'

'No, no!' she said, sagging against him and trying hard to stifle a yawn.

'Yes!'

'Well, maybe,' she conceded with a smile.

'Definitely, not maybe. I'll show you where everything is. Then you can climb into bed and settle down.'

'Will you come as well?'

'In a little while. I need to sort out one or two things first. Don't you worry about me or anything else, though. You've been through enough. Get some rest. We'll talk tomorrow.'

She smiled that little smile he remembered so well, and said, 'Thank you, John. You're so understanding, and I feel so safe with you.'

In truth, he didn't have much to do. He just wasn't ready for sleep, but he knew Vlasta was. She was out on her feet. Not just from the recent travelling, either. She had been living on her nerves too long. Even before her father was blitzed she had been doing that. He couldn't begin to imagine what it had been like since then.

One thing he knew, though: all that was over. He was determined about that. They were going to live a different kind of life from now on, and find a better way of living. He didn't want any more of the excitement people like Viktor Sirko provided. He just hoped Vlasta didn't, either. It wasn't worth it.

The move on Vlasta in London had unsettled him more than a bit. He hadn't really thought it likely, although he had known something like that was certainly possible. Fortunately, he had been on guard and able to deal with it. He wondered if she had been spotted at the airport in Kiev, and the information passed on to people in London. These organizations — and you had to call them that, these organized crime syndicates — had widespread networks, thanks to the internet and the so-called global economy.

But how far could they really reach? London, obviously, but London was a bit special. It wasn't all of England, never mind the whole of the United Kingdom. It was just the place where most of the Russian diaspora was located. Here, Northumberland, was different. And long may it remain so.

On that note, he went to bed, where he found that Vlasta was already fast asleep.

The next morning, over breakfast, the debriefing began. At least, that was what it seemed like. There was so much information to exchange, and they simply couldn't wait any longer to get started. By then, Vlasta was rested and more like her old self. The anxiety and fatigue had almost gone from her face.

Accepting another cup of coffee from him, she smiled, glanced around the kitchen and said, 'This is a very nice house, John. How did you find it? What are you doing here, anyway, so far from London?'

He gave her a rueful smile. 'Would you believe me if I said it was a long story?'

'Oh, yes!' she said, laughing. 'I am sure it is a very long story.'

'Well . . . Not so long, really, I suppose. I visited this area a couple of times when I was a child. My grandmother lived here. I always remembered it as a happy place, and a happy time. So when I needed a port of refuge, this was where came to mind. After I got back to England, I more or less came straight here and found somewhere to live.' He smiled at her and added, 'Sometimes I despaired of ever seeing you again, Vlasta, but I knew that if I did, I would like you to consider being here with me. That's a decision for you to take, of course, and you must take your time. There's no hurry. But it is what I hope will happen. First, though, there are things I need to tell you.'

She nodded agreement.

'At least for now, we know we can live here safely.'

She looked at him curiously for a moment and said, 'John, is there something you are perhaps not telling me?'

He nodded. 'Quite a lot, actually,' he admitted with a rueful smile, 'but all that can wait. I want to hear what went on back there in Lviv.'

She pulled a face.

'Tell you what,' he said, 'let's go for a little walk. Get some fresh air. You can tell me some of it as we go.'

It had been every bit as bad as he had feared. Yugov, Viktor Sirko's Russian nemesis, had hit hard and suddenly, and with devastating power. The strike in Lviv had been only one part of it. That had been intended to behead the Sirko business empire, and put an end to any possibility of it ever recovering, which it had certainly done. But the main thrust had been in the east, in Donetsk and elsewhere in the old industrial belt. "The Rust Bucket", as Sirko had habitually referred to it, even though the old steel and heavy engineering industries there were an important part of his empire.

Viktor Sirko had been assassinated, and many others killed in his HQ staff in Lviv. Vlasta wasn't aware of any senior figures in the organization who had been able to escape. That made John even more aware of how lucky he had been. He was still wondering how it had happened.

'Where were you when you phoned to warn me?'

'I was fortunate,' Vlasta said with a sigh. 'I had been out of town, to visit friends in a nearby village. Father was also out of town. He was travelling — maybe to Kiev, but I'm not sure.'

'Further east. Kharkiv, I think,' John said automatically, remembering Viktor's schedule.

'Yes. You're right. Kharkiv. Anyway, Yugov's people caught him in an ambush on the road. I don't know the details. He phoned me while it was still happening. Nothing much. Just a simple, quick call to say there was an emergency.

'He told me not to go back to the offices. It wouldn't be safe. If we didn't see each other again, he said to remember that he loved me.'

Tears streamed down her face. John stopped walking to hug her. She clung to him desperately.

Later, alongside the river, she paused and pointed. 'Look, John. Ducks!'

'Mallards,' he said, pretending to believe in her show of happiness. 'They make a good living along here from all the bread people bring them. That old swan does, too.'

She looked across to the other side of the river, where a swan was sailing along serenely, not a care in the world.

'It's so peaceful here,' she said with wonder. 'Like it used to be in my country.'

When was that, he wondered. Not this century, nor the last. Not the one before that, either. But he said nothing. He had no wish to disrupt her brave attempt to be happy. Besides, there was still so much that he wanted to know.

'So that was why you could warn me?' he said. 'Because your father had already called you?'

She nodded. 'I knew what would happen next. This wasn't a pinprick. If they were targeting Father, this was the major offensive he had always suspected would happen one day. He knew the Russians wanted control of his industries in the east, and would go to any lengths to get them. So I knew it would be best if you got out while you still could. And you did,' she added gravely, turning away from the river to gaze directly at him.

'I did, thanks to you. At first I thought it was a joke, but then I saw Yugov's men arrive in trucks. There were a lot of them. There was nothing I could do. I was unarmed. They had heavy weapons. It was all over so quickly. So I just ran,' he said with a sigh.

She took his arm and said, 'Tell me where you went.'

CHAPTER TWELVE

He told her about the mad dash out of Ukraine and into Slovakia. He told her about his flight across central and western Europe, and back to England. She listened patiently, taking it all in carefully. Then she asked him what he had had with him when he made his escape.

'Nothing, almost nothing,' he said. 'Just a passport, which I always carried.'

'You didn't return to the flat?'

'No. It would have been too big a risk. I saw with my own eyes what they were doing. I wasn't in any doubt what would happen if they found me. I wasn't important, but that wouldn't have made any difference. They weren't stopping to ask questions. It was like watching the old Red Army on the move. Hit hard and destroy.

'You saved me, Vlasta. I would have been in the main building when they arrived if you hadn't called.'

She nodded and stopped walking to gaze across the village green. 'It's so beautiful here,' she said. 'So serene. Is that the right word?'

'It could be,' he admitted with a grin, surprised by the fluency of her English. 'But just wait till the kids get out of school!'

She laughed. He was glad to hear her. Their conversation had become almost oppressive to him, and he knew it was a long way from over.

'Coffee?' he asked. 'There's a little tea shop where they serve good coffee — and a cheese scone, if you fancy one?'

'Cheese scone?' She savoured the sound of it. 'I don't know that word.'

'Almost a delicacy in the north of England,' he assured her.

She nodded thoughtfully and then said, 'I would like that. But there is something else, isn't there? You are not telling me everything, John. Only what you think I need to know, perhaps?'

He smiled ruefully. 'Can't fool you, can I?'

'Not if we are to be together, John,' she said firmly. 'I need to know everything. No secrets. Remember?'

Indeed he did remember. They had not been lovers for long, him and the boss's daughter, but it had been long enough. They had walked across egg shells, he ultra-careful to avoid giving offence, she not sure how a relationship with him could work in her father's world. But they had promised to be honest with each other, always. It was the only way.

'You got out fast,' she continued. 'After I called, you had perhaps minutes to escape. So you got out with only what you had in your pockets at the time, and yet you travelled across Europe and reached here so quickly. How? There must be something I don't know. Am I right?'

So now he told her about the dead man in the ski lodge in Slovakia, and he told her about the money. He had wanted to wait until he was sure she was fully recovered from her ordeal, and for a time when they were used to each other again, but he hadn't reckoned with Vlasta's intuitive ability to understand what lay beneath the surface. That was her father's legacy.

She nodded now and said, 'I knew there must be something you were not telling me.'

'It seemed too soon. I wanted to wait until you were more settled.'

'It is better this way, I think.'

'Coffee?'

'In just a moment, John.'

Still pondering what he had told her, she said, 'The man who was murdered. You have no idea who he was?'

'None at all. I don't even know what nationality he was, not that that matters very much.'

'But he was an arms salesman?'

'That was my guess, but I don't know for sure.'

'Someone will know.'

'Perhaps they will,' he said sharply, 'but it was nothing to do with me. It isn't now, either. I don't even want to know!'

She shook her head, dissatisfied. 'It is strange that who-ever killed him left the money.'

'Either the killer was under orders or didn't have the time or inclination to look.'

'But someone will be looking for the money,' she pointed out.

He shrugged. 'Who knows? They could be. But there was a little war going on in Lviv, and things disappear in wartime.'

'You have it here with you?'

'I have it, but not here. And before you ask me what I'm going to do with it, I have to tell you I don't know. As of yet, I haven't been able to think of a safe way of using it.'

He told her then about the difficulties of using money irregularly gained without raising the suspicions, or worse, of organized criminals or the authorities.

'I could have found people in London who would have laundered the money for me — found ways of investing it.'

'But you didn't?'

He shook his head. 'Once you do that, someone knows who you are, and what you've got. You can always be found, if they have a good enough reason to search. I didn't want to risk that. This way is safer.'

'It is true.' Vlasta nodded approval. 'You did the right thing, John.'

'I have used some of the money, of course,' he said. 'Small amounts. I had no choice. Leaving as I did meant I had to leave everything behind. I came out with ten euros in my pocket.'

'I know how that is,' Vlasta admitted. 'I, too, lost almost everything. To buy a ticket to come here, I had to sell a gold locket my father gave me.' Looking him firmly in the eye, she added, 'It is best not to spend the money, John. We didn't earn it, and spending it would draw attention to us. Leave it where it is. Let us live simply, and safely. We will find some honest way of making our living.'

'That's my thinking,' he said.

He hung on to the "we" in her suggestion. Did it mean she would stay, stay for good?

'Coffee now, Vlasta?'

'Yes, thank you. That would be good.'

'If you are ready,' he said slowly, 'I can talk to you about how we might make that honest living. I have an idea.'

CHAPTER THIRTEEN

It was an old ruin, a building that had once been a well-endowed house. Now it had walls, but not much else. The roof had gone, as had the windows and doors. The floors were simply rubble. But the stream still burbled past the bottom of what had once been the garden, and there were trees to provide shelter from winter winds. All in all, it was a charming location. Idly, he wondered what it would cost to fix the house. A lot of money. That was for sure.

Late that evening, he thought, well, I have a lot of money! What better to do with a small part of it than rebuild something, make a tangible improvement to the world?

Go for it? Why not!

Just like that, the idea he had long been searching for had come to him.

The problem of how to make use of the money that had fallen into his possession had exercised him since day one, well before Vlasta came on the scene. It didn't seem possible in a legal sense. There were so many constraints in this security-conscious age, with its fear of terrorism and its clamp-down on money laundering opportunities.

Besides, he wasn't sure he really wanted to use the money. Some of it, for necessities, perhaps. Just to get him started. But no more. He didn't want to start feeling like a retired crime boss living on dirty money. He had never been overly scrupulous, but he had always had an instinctive feel for decent ethical standards and had tried to keep to them.

And he did need to do something with his life. He wanted to work and earn, just as he always had done. So self-respect came into it, along with personal honour. Idleness didn't appeal very much at all, once he had got the first few weeks out of his system. He needed, craved, a sense of purpose.

Redundancy and enforced idleness, after being made redundant from a branch of military intelligence, was why he had gone to work for Viktor Sirko in the first place. Well, that and a craving for something new, and for the chance to explore a country he had never visited.

Viktor had not found him difficult to persuade when they had bumped into each other on a holiday in Montenegro. Both mountain lovers, they had taken to each other instantly, and the rest had followed as easily as night follows day. Two good and hard years he'd had with Viktor until the barbarians had arrived from the east, in the traditional way.

So for some time he had thought long and hard about what to do now, without coming up with anything very appealing. The answer only came with his discovery of the old ruined house.

He asked in the village pub who owned it, as the landlord seemed to know everything and everybody.

'Down by the river? That old cottage, you mean?'

He nodded.

'Danny!' the landlord said, turning round. 'Bloke here wants to know who owns that ruined cottage of yours.'

A man along at the other end of the bar turned, looked surprised for a moment and then chuckled. '*Primrose Cottage*? Thinking of buying it, is he?'

'I don't know. Ask him yourself.'

John grinned, entering into the spirit of things, and moved along the bar. 'I was just asking who owns it,' he said. 'So it's yours, is it?'

'If it's the same one. Along the river, near where the beck comes in?'

John nodded.

'Well, I suppose I do own it, such as it is. It was my granny's cottage. Mind you, she wouldn't recognize it now. It's fallen to bits over the past half century.'

'It's a pity. It's a lovely location.'

'If you like that sort of thing. Danny Nelson, by the way,' the man added, holding out a hand.

'John Tait.'

'Looking for somewhere to live, are you?' Danny asked with a grin. 'I don't think that would be much good to you.'

'No, not really. I've got a house in the village. But I was thinking somebody would enjoy living there again, if it was done up a bit.'

'Aye, well. One day, maybe. If someone offers me money for it, I'll grab their hand off. I will!'

John thought about that. He thought about it a lot. The ruin became something of an obsession with him, probably because he had little else to do. He could imagine how it used to be, and how it could be again — if only someone with interest, and the money to back it up, came on the scene.

Finally, he went back to Danny Nelson and asked him how much he would want for it. Twenty grand was the answer. Done!

That was how it all started.

He arranged to pay Danny Nelson in cash, part in advance and part in monthly instalments over the next several years — or until such time as the purchase price could be paid in full, in one go. He made similar arrangements with an architect in Alnwick and a builder from up the valley who was short of work.

Paying in small amounts at a time, he could pay cash. That suited everyone, himself most of all. It was as if the money was coming from his revenue stream, rather than a storage unit in Wallsend.

When the cottage was habitable again, he put it on the market. A couple of months later it sold for nearly £200,000, and he could pay off his debts in one go.

At that point, he announced to the local branch of his bank that he was a business start-up, and wanted to open a business account alongside his personal account. What kind of business? Property development. The bank was delighted to oblige.

Then he looked for another property to restore, using the profit from the sale of the first one to part-finance another purchase. It was the start of a continuing process that he found rewarding, both financially and personally.

By the time Vlasta came on the scene, he had a nice little business going, one that satisfied his need to be usefully employed, and one that he hoped might even appeal to Vlasta. It did.

'That's your big idea?' Vlasta said with a smile.

'It is. What do you think?'

'I think it's wonderful, John! Buy old houses, repair them and then sell them again?'

'That's the idea.'

'And we do this together?'

He nodded. 'I've made a start, but together we could do more. I thought you might like to become the interior design partner.'

She laughed. 'That would be a challenge. But, yes, I like the idea. How clever you are to have started all this!'

'Well, having the money helped.'

Her face fell. 'Ah! The money. What happens to that now? Will we need to use it?'

He shook his head. 'Not now. The business generates its own money now it's got going. I've scarcely touched it.'

'So what will we do with it?'

'I don't know.' He shrugged. 'For now, at least, let's just do as you suggested, and leave it where it is — in storage.'

Vlasta agreed. 'That will be best, I think. This is a simple village. We will not need such a lot of money to live well here.'

'So you want to stay?'

'Of course,' she said sharply. 'To be with you. It is why I came here. Did you doubt me?'

'No, no!' he said with relief, and with a smile. 'I just wanted to be sure.'

'Now you can be,' she said sternly.

A few months later, they obtained a mortgage that enabled them to buy the first home of their own, and they left the rented cottage where John had first found refuge and that had served them both so well.

It was at that time that Vlasta told John she believed it would be better for her, and for them, if she took an English name. Her own name made her feel too conspicuous. He began to argue, and then stopped himself.

'You've been thinking about this, haven't you?' he said.

She nodded. 'I would like to be called Samantha,' she said. 'Sam, for short, I believe?'

He nodded and grinned. 'So I have another new woman in my life?'

'No, no!' she said. 'The same old one.'

Three years later, when Kyle was born, he believed they had it all now. Life was good. Vlasta — or Sam, as he was used to calling her by then — smiled and agreed. Their course was set. Her homeland was a long way behind them both. Or so they thought.

CHAPTER FOURTEEN

The English Borders, Northumberland, 10 September 2014

George Riley had never been to Northern England before. He had been to London many times, and to smaller towns in Kent and the Thames Valley. He had been to Edinburgh, too. But Northern England was terra incognito so far as he was concerned. His view from the window of the plane as it came into land at Newcastle Airport suggested that what he had heard about this part of the country was pretty accurate. Cold, cloudy and wet summed it up very well.

He picked up a four-wheel drive Toyota from the Hertz depot at the airport and headed up country. He knew where he was going. Ted had given him the address, and he had a couple of maps. He was headed for a village in a valley, where he had booked himself a room in a hotel. Not far. Less than an hour's drive, probably.

The King's Arms wasn't too bad, he decided. He could live with it. His room was basic, but it had what he needed. The restaurant was OK, too. Maybe the steaks were a little on the small and thin side, but that was good for him. He'd been putting on weight the past year or two. So it was OK here. He'd been in plenty worse places than this.

The landlord said, 'We get a lot of you people through here.'

'That right?'

The comment made him wonder what kind of people he was. It disappointed him, as well. He didn't like being noticed when he was on a job.

'Yanks. Americans. They come for the history mostly. Castles and battlefields. Things like that. They certainly don't come for the weather!'

Riley smiled agreeably and made a suitable comment. He was standing at the bar, waiting for the landlord to complete pumping him a glass of English beer. Just then, he was the only customer. Early evening, too.

'None here tonight, though?'

The landlord pursed his lips and shook his head. 'No Germans, either. We get a lot of them as well. Nobody else here at all, in fact. It's quiet during the week, especially at this time of year. In fact,' he added, 'it's pretty quiet most of the time these days. The drink driving campaign and the ban on smoking have seen to that. The supermarkets haven't helped, either, the prices they charge for beer. Country pubs don't have much future, in my opinion. Not unless they can build a good food trade, which not all of them can do.'

'Bad as that, is it?'

The landlord nodded. 'Mind you,' he went on, 'the villages don't have a lot of anything these days. Used to be the case that a village would have a garage, a pub, a post office, a couple of shops. Nowadays plenty of villages have nothing at all. Even the churches are closing down.'

'What about this village?'

'Oh, this one isn't so bad. We've still got a village shop, as well as this pub. The shop sells pretty much everything. Although, there isn't a post office anymore.'

Riley nodded thoughtfully, as if he cared, and sat himself down on a bar stool. He could learn stuff here, but it looked like being a long night.

He spent a couple of days familiarizing himself with the village and the surrounding area. It was a small village, surrounded by open moorland — as he understood they called the heather-clad hills in the area — and little copses of scots pine that provided shelter for deer and game birds. The handful of farms within a five-mile radius were all hill sheep farms, the sheep roaming wild over the moors most of the year.

The village itself was mostly in the valley, on both sides of the river, with a few houses spreading along a couple of roads up the valley sides. The address he had been given was on one of those roads, on the north side of the river. It was a pleasant looking detached house with a lot of garden. Maybe a hundred years old. Built of local stone. Not big, but big enough for a small family.

That was what seemed to live in the house: a small family. There was a woman and a young boy, as well as the man. That seemed to be it.

Well, Riley thought philosophically, the woman was going to have to find another man, and the kid another dad. This one had had his card marked. Too bad.

The thought didn't bother him for a moment. He'd been too long in the saddle for that. All he was concerned with was the guy, and completing the mission. Then he would be out of here, never to return. Back to the woods he knew so well.

But first he had checks to make. He had to make sure this was the right guy.

Tait. John Tait. That was his name.

He was nothing special to look at. Medium height and build, medium coloured hair — medium everything, in fact. Late thirties, probably. Fit enough, seemingly, but nothing special. Just ordinary. Like the best of the Special Forces guys, he just looked ordinary.

Riley had seen the type often enough. He knew what guys who looked like this could do. He wasn't fooled by appearances. But as he watched the Tait household for a couple of days, he became puzzled. This wasn't what he had expected. He needed to take his time, and be careful. He needed to get it right.

He could see Tait as Jack Olsson's killer, all right. That wasn't a problem. But for a guy who had strolled off with $10,000,000 afterwards, he didn't exactly live in style. His house was OK, but nothing special, like him.

Also, he had a job, some sort of business. He was a builder, for chrissake! The guy fixed up old houses. Hard work, and not a lot of money in it. If he had $10,000,000, why do it?

CHAPTER FIFTEEN

Riley walked on the moor above the north side of the village, deep in thought. This Tait guy, he just didn't look right somehow. Was he really the one who had whacked Jack Olsson? It was hard to see it.

This guy just didn't seem like someone who — admittedly ten years ago — had been a hitman on the loose in Slovakia and Ukraine. His life wasn't like that. Not now, at least. It might have been once, he supposed, but . . . really? Tait?

The evidence trail had led Ted Pearson to Tait, but Riley still felt he needed more than that. He wanted confirmation based on other evidence before he blew the guy away. He needed to do due diligence on him. Ted would expect that, too.

While he was here, Ted had also suggested, it would be good if he could find out what had happened to the money. Maybe even recover some of it. Fat chance! He'd seen nothing to suggest it was here. This Tait guy was working his butt off just to feed his family. He wasn't living out of a money bag taken from Jack Olsson.

A quarter of a mile away there was a slope covered in gorse. From there, you had a good view of the Tait house. Riley had been up there once or twice before, watching, getting a feel for the movement pattern of the Tait household. He headed there now, making his way through deep heather.

The ground was sodden, and the heather dripping with drizzle and condensation. A stream would have taken some of the surplus water away, but there were no streams up here on the moor. They didn't start until springs erupted from the ground halfway down the hillside. But once started, they tumbled their way rapidly down to the valley, and a river that was already at bank-full stage. It was wet country, now at least.

Cold and wet, and gloomy as it was up here, Riley could cope. He was used to hunting in the woods, and where he lived conditions were not much different to this in the fall. Colder, if anything. There was no sign of snow here, but back home it could well be happening already. So he knew how to dress and equip himself for these conditions. The story he'd put out in the King's Arms was that he was a bird watcher, here for the autumn migrations. That meant no one raised an eyebrow about his wet weather gear.

The Tait household, so far at least, had stuck to a pretty regular routine. Nothing out of the ordinary at all. They stirred shortly before seven in the morning. Lights went on. Shadows moved behind closed drapes. Mum and Dad were busy.

Soon after seven, Tait would take himself off in his truck, a battered old Ford that had seen better days, and head out to a house he was working on a few miles away. Riley knew where he was going because he had followed him there a couple of times. In his opinion the guy had taken on a lot of work.

Sometimes Tait was joined by a couple of other guys, depending on what stage the work was at, and if he needed to bring in specialist skills. Mostly, though, he was there all day long, just himself — working like a fucking trojan! Working like a guy who didn't have $10,000,000 in the bank.

Around 8.30 a.m., the woman took the kid to school. If it was fine, and they were in good time, they walked. Once or twice, when the weather was piss poor or somebody hadn't been able to get out of bed that morning, she took him in her little car. Responsible behaviour. Looking after the boy. Doing what mums did the world over, every day of their fucking lives.

Once junior was in school, the woman sometimes headed to the village shop. Occasionally, she got in her car and kept going, out to the nearest big town, a few miles away, where they had supermarkets. Or she might call in to see the guy — her husband, or whatever he was — to encourage him, share a laugh, eat a lunchtime sandwich. Nothing special going on, so far as Riley could see.

After supper they would usually be at home. Tait would no doubt count the money he'd taken from Jack Olsson all over again. Maybe. What the fuck had he done with it? Had he really got it? Was it really him even?

This was doing his head in. If Tait ever had been an operator in eastern Europe, he certainly wasn't now. He could see no connection at all. The hitman, if that was what he had been, was retired. Hell of a retirement, though. Working harder than ever.

Still, retired or not, according to Ted Pearson, this was the guy who killed Jack Olsson. So he had to go. Better get on with it. He'd seen all there was to see. He'd done due diligence, and found no big surprises. Just little ones. Nothing to say this wasn't the right guy, even if he didn't seem to fit very well.

Time to get the job done, and get back home. He'd just have to tell Ted the money must have been spent long ago. There was no sign of it now.

Hell, $10,000,000? What was that anyway? Not worth even thinking about, back there in DC. Every time they fired off a cruise missile, or another drone strike on some foreign fellows wearing sandals, that was another million dollars spent. And, God knew, there had been enough of them things launched in the past few years.

This particular morning, Riley settled into his position amongst the gorse. He could take the guy out from here, and would do it soon with the rifle Ted had got to him by special courier. Nothing to it. Easy shot. And he was just about ready to go.

No need to get up any closer. Well, not unless he was going to ask Tait why he'd killed Jack Olsson, and what he'd done with the money. Hell, if he was going to do that, he might as well ask him what he'd been doing in Slovakia in the first place! Before he shot him, that is.

But his heart wasn't really in this job anymore. He wasn't in investigative mode. He just wanted to get it done, and then get home. He didn't believe Ted was that concerned about the money. Petty cash, in Washington terms. It would have been marked off and forgotten long ago. Miscellaneous expenditure. If there was any still hidden away somewhere, the woman could keep it for herself and the kid. They would need it.

All Ted, and the service, really wanted out of this was to know that Jack Olsson's killer had not got away with it. Had, in fact, paid with his life. That was what he wanted as well. It was why he was here.

So hit the guy. Then he and, soon, Ted, too, could get on with their lives in retirement, with Jack avenged, honour satisfied, and the bad guy taken off the board.

He started fitting the rifle together.

The cloud hung heavily on the moor that morning. Puffs of it came and went with unseen eddies of cool, damp air. Visibility was poor. The scope he was using kept clouding up. Every half minute or so he had to wipe the lens clear. Sometimes the damned thing was misleading him. Sometimes he imagined he was seeing movement in a small pinewood up to the left, just above the Tait place.

Shit! There was movement. It wasn't his imagination.

He cleaned the scope again and re-focused it carefully. Yep. Someone there, all right. A guy. And — would you believe it? — he was studying the Tait house through field glasses.

Riley frowned. What the hell was this? Competition? Someone else wanting revenge, or to know what had happened to all them bucks?

He kept the scope focused on the pinewood. It was definitely a guy. Just the one. And he was watching, just as he was himself.

He pulled out a camera and with the zoom lens took a few photos of the watcher, his face only partly obscured by twigs and branches.

Ten minutes later, the guy moved back through the pinewood and disappeared. Riley stayed where he was for some time after that, deep in thought, ignoring the rain that had begun to fall steadily now and was coming across the hillside in hissing sheets.

This altered things. It could be a game changer. Someone else interested in Tait. A rival outfit? Or was it a repeat burglary? Ted had told him about the burglary earlier that year. A voyeur even, hoping to catch sight of Tait's wife coming out of the shower? What the hell was it?

Impossible to know. But it did alter things. Demanded more thought, more time. He would put things on hold. Something unexpected was going on. He needed to know what it was before he pulled the trigger.

A half hour later, he began to ease himself back through the thicket of gorse. There was nothing more he could learn from here. He needed to look elsewhere. In the meantime, he would send his photos back to Ted in DC, and see if the people there could come up with a name to go with the face.

CHAPTER SIXTEEN

The next day started off just the same, weatherwise. The drizzle was incessant, and the low cloud didn't look like lifting at all. It would be another cold, wet day on the moor. Riley donned his wet weather gear again and set out to maintain his vigil once more.

The day started off normally for the Taits, which he found surprising given the watcher he'd spotted the previous day. Back then, he'd wondered if something out of the ordinary was about to kick off, but it hadn't. Not yet, at least.

The Tait family got up, had breakfast and went about their business. Tait himself set off in his truck again to the house he was working on. The woman got herself and the boy ready, and then took the boy to school. After that, she did a bit of shopping in the village before visiting someone who lived near the pub, probably for coffee.

That was when Riley decided to switch his focus back to Tait. He set off for the building project.

It was an old stone farmhouse where Tait was working. Riley's guess was that it had been empty a long, long time. The roof had collapsed, in part, and the chimney stack looked ready to fall in the next high wind. High grass and scrub had grown right up to the front doorway, and in the nearby shelter belt of scots pine there were a lot of fallen trees. Tait had his work cut out, and so far had not made a lot of progress. Much hard work and patience were going to be required, in Riley's humble opinion.

He left his car a good half mile away, in a layby the highway authority had earmarked as a good place to store gravel for maintenance purposes. He walked around the edge of a couple of fields and made his way into the woodland near the house.

Then he settled down to wait, keeping one eye on the house, where Tait was busy clearing out debris and fallen timbers. With the other eye, with his ears and with a sniper's extra sensitivity, he monitored his surroundings constantly, searching for anything that shouldn't rightly be there.

Mid-morning it happened again. He was just beginning to wonder if he was wasting his time. Thinking maybe he should call it a day, ice Tait and get the hell out. That was when he spotted two guys watching Tait from behind a hedge alongside the road, some distance away. They didn't stay long. And nothing else happened. But it was enough. He knew now for sure that he had competition — and that Tait was in even greater trouble.

The day after that was different almost from the start. The Taits got up and made themselves ready for the day, as usual. But when Tait left the house he was wearing a dark business suit and he slipped into a saloon car, a VW Passat, instead of climbing into his old truck. Then he took off fast, seemingly in a hurry to have a different kind of day for once.

Riley grimaced. He had been caught flat-footed. He hadn't expected anything like that. What the hell was the guy up to?

He stayed where he was for a while, wondering what the rest of the family was going to do today. The same old thing, it looked like. At 8.30 a.m., the woman and kid emerged, and set off for the school. Reassuringly, it looked like being a normal day for them.

There was no sign of anyone else watching the family home. He gave it a good couple of hours before withdrawing from cover, but no one else had appeared in that time.

None of the Taits had come home, either. The house was empty.

He hung around all day, checking back periodically, but nothing else happened to or around the Tait place. The guy was gone, somewhere. The boy was in school. The woman was out shopping, and visiting. That was it. Nothing out of the ordinary.

Riley did some thinking, and he did some more wandering around the village and the surrounding area. The place was beginning to feel familiar to him, but there was always some little corner he hadn't explored. That day he spent some time in and around the eleventh century church, admiring the stone carvings and the wood panelling, the tombstones and the ancient yew trees. Then in late afternoon, he returned to his station on the hillside, ready to resume his watch on the Taits, and curious to see if anyone else showed up.

They didn't.

And that was how it was for the next few days. Tait was gone somewhere. His family carried on as usual. Riley spotted no one else watching the house.

But late one afternoon everything changed. The woman and the boy didn't return home, and the house remained dark as night fell.

CHAPTER SEVENTEEN

George Riley waited with the patience of a sniper. Something had happened, and he knew from experience that once things started happening they didn't stop. So he waited a long time. He waited until John Tait came home. By then, it was early evening, and getting dark.

Tait seemed out of sorts. It was soon clear that he didn't like the house being empty. This was unexpected. He went through every room repeatedly, looking for something. Looking for them, probably. Looking for his family.

Riley could guess the next step. He didn't need to stay any longer. So he slipped away and made his way back to where he had left the car, shaking and flexing to shake off the stiffness as he went. It had been a long day.

He was past his best for this kind of thing. One time it wouldn't have bothered him, sitting still for half a day. He could have waited two or three days in a row, longer even, if necessary, without stirring or being particularly uncomfortable. Not now, though. Half a day now, and he could feel the arthritis stirring, making itself felt in his back and in his knees.

Not in his arms or hands, though, thank God. Once that happened, he really would be over the hill. You couldn't be a sniper any more, or much of a hunter either, once your hands and fingers turned stiff on you.

He drove into the village and sat and waited there. Sure enough, Tait's car soon appeared. Then Tait started checking around, visiting the school and different shops, looking for them. Looking for his family. Unable to understand why they were not where they should be.

Something had happened, obviously. Some crisis or emergency? But if it was that, surely there would have been a message or a clue left by somebody?

Riley pursed his lips and thought about it. Tait had not been expecting this. His wife and son were not where he had expected them to be, and he was deeply upset, verging on panicked. But why?

His guess was that it was something to do with whoever else it was watching Tait and his house. Had they abducted the woman and the boy? It was beginning to seem possible. He couldn't think of anything else that fit the bill.

Whether or not that had happened, though, all this running around like a headless chicken indicated to Riley's satisfaction that Tait was indeed the guy. Ted, and his sources, had got it right, after all.

But he still wasn't ready to take him out. Not yet. He wanted to know what was going on before he did that. Being in possession of only half the picture never was satisfactory.

While he was waiting to see what Tait did next, a call from base came in on his phone.

'How's it going, George?'

'OK, Ted. Just going through the checks. Making sure.'

'Right. Those photos you sent?'

'Yeah?'

'You wanted a name. Try Alexei Kuznetsov. That fit?'

'Dunno. Should it?'

'He works for Vassily Yugov.'

'Yugov?' George said with surprise. 'It's been a while since I last heard that name mentioned.'

'Yeah, well. Me, too.'

'Don't tell me he's around?'

'It looks like he could be.'

'Know any reason why?'

'Not offhand, no.'

Yugov, he thought afterwards. That bastard! What was his interest in Tait?

Olsson's $10,000,000? It was very possible.

Maybe he was someone else who had linked Tait to events in Ukraine and Slovakia all those years ago. In his case, though, it would be the money trail he was following. Yugov wouldn't be worrying over who killed Jack Olsson back then, or looking to get even, either.

Yugov, eh? Well, well. That was something else for him to think about. The job he had come to do no longer seemed quite so simple. He gave a wry smile. Hadn't it always been like that?

Riley returned to his hide on the hillside. The rain eased off for a while, and then came back again stronger than ever. I'm getting too old for this, he thought, listening to it pattering on his waterproof hat. Correction: I am too old for it!

But he stayed where he was. Things had got more interesting. A hot shower, a hot meal and a hot, dry bed were certainly appealing, but something was going on here now. He didn't want to miss it. If he hit Tait now, he never would find out what it was.

He was reasonably comfortable. Warm, and dry inside. He had a bottle of water and a couple of sandwiches. He never had needed much more when he was on a job. Even more in his favour, in the dark he could stretch and move without risking giving away his position.

Beyond that, he still had the stoicism demanded by his old trade. He could sit and watch, almost without movement, for a long, long time, even now.

The lights went out in the house shortly before midnight. That was when it got even more interesting. A big SUV vehicle arrived in the drive and parked behind Tait's car, blocking it in. Four men got out and moved towards the house.

Then some sort of scuffle developed in the shadows beside the house. Figures spilled and sprawled in all directions. One broke free and headed at speed not towards the vehicles in the driveway but down the garden. Three others followed.

When the first figure passed under an external light at the back of the house, Riley could see it was Tait, moving fast. He reached the bottom of the garden, scrambled over the wall and began to run at the hillside, heading up towards the moor.

For a moment, Riley wondered if he had been spotted. Then he saw that Tait was taking a line that would bypass him by fifty yards or so. The figures following Tait were also running now.

He was fascinated. Although the light was too poor for him to have seen everything that had happened, he had seen enough to believe he wasn't the only one who wanted Tait dead.

For a few minutes, he had even felt superfluous to requirements. The competition had come in a gang of four, more than enough, he would have thought, to take out one man. But it hadn't worked out that way. Not yet, at least.

Through his night-vision scope he had watched the shadowy drama unfold. As Tait's visitors neared the back door of the house, the door swung open and Tait erupted explosively to lay into them without hesitation or inhibition. One man went down instantly. The others were hurled aside as if by a hurricane force. Within seconds, the ground was clear and Tait was speeding for the hillside.

Riley nodded, muttered something incomprehensible and clenched his fist, caught up in the sudden violence.

It looked as if Ted Pearson had been right all along. This was the guy. As he'd noted before, Tait wasn't much to look at in a physical sense, but he had the mental and physical strength and the power of a Special Forces soldier. He'd just shown how capable he was. So this probably was the man who had hit Jack Olsson all those years back. Whatever he'd been doing since that time, he hadn't lost much of his capability.

He watched and listened to Tait powering his way up the hillside for a few moments. Then he turned his attention back to the men who had come to do him harm. Three of them were back on their feet now. One stopped briefly to look at the fourth, who was still flat on his back. There was a brief conversation between those on their feet. A quick phone call followed. Then they set off after Tait.

Riley quickly considered his own options, and decided to go with the pack. He wanted to see what happened next. But he wasn't going to run.

CHAPTER EIGHTEEN

Tait was stunned by the phone call. When the phone went dead, he slumped against the wall for a few moments, fighting against the despair and panic that were threatening to overwhelm him. This was the nightmare returning, the one he had fought to suppress and deny all these years. It was back. Only it wasn't actually a nightmare; it was real this time.

He knew who they were, all right. And he knew what they wanted. After all this time!

He thumped the wall with frustration. When that failed to make it all go away, he banged his head hard against the wall. Same thing. No difference at all.

What the hell could he do? He waited for another call. It didn't come. He wandered around the house, waiting, trying to get some sort of control, trying to calm down and think rationally.

When he managed to stop beating himself up he returned to the kitchen, where he drew the blinds and switched on the kettle to make himself a coffee.

Then something occurred to him that he should have thought of earlier. Why hadn't they told him their demands? Why hadn't they proposed a deal — his wife and son in exchange for the money?

He thought about that, and came to a welcome conclusion: they hadn't got them! They couldn't have. His wife and son were not in their hands.

If they had got them, they would simply have told him to hand the money over if he wanted his family back. They hadn't. So Sam and Kyle must be out there somewhere, in the night, free but unable to come home or let him know what had happened.

He could be wrong, but the more he thought about it, the more he didn't think so. It was the only explanation that made sense. Sam must have seen something, and at the first hint of danger she would have grabbed Kyle and run. Knowing her, she would probably have taken to the hills, as she had occasionally joked she would do if necessary. Until now, it never had been necessary, but now was different.

So he knew now what he had to do. He would search for them, and find them — and keep them safe. It was as simple as that.

Hurriedly, but with steady purpose, he ranged through the house, collecting what he needed. Into a backpack went stuff he hadn't used for years, but that once had been familiar to him as basic survival gear.

He changed his clothes, donning wet weather gear. What about Sam and Kyle? They could be in need of warm, dry clothing, too, but he had to balance that likelihood against consideration of the weight he would be carrying. Speed over the ground was going to be essential.

The grim reality, in this weather, was that if they were out there and he didn't find them soon, they wouldn't need dry clothing — or anything else, either. Hypothermia would have taken its toll.

Gloves, boots and socks were what he packed for them. They were going to have to manage with whatever else they were wearing. Hopefully, that included decent outdoor jackets with hoods.

He added a small stove with a fuel cell to his pack. And then mess tins and a couple of mugs. Some dried food packets. No water, though. There was plenty of that out there.

All the time, his mental clock was running. He had been packing for fifteen minutes, fifteen precious minutes. It was long enough. He had to get moving.

Finally, he went to the emergency cache and took out passports and money. He also took the Glock pistol he had acquired from a dead man in Slovakia all those years ago, along with ammunition for it.

A pause for a final quick think. Then he was out the door, striding into the night, and the wind and rain, heading for the hills. He was gambling. Of all the places Sam could have taken Kyle, he was opting for the one that was most difficult to reach, the one she would feel was safest.

But it wasn't as simple as that. As soon as he was outside, he saw the car arrive. They were coming for him. Four of them. He had no doubt who, or what, they were. As they approached, he reached sideways, grabbed a short length of scaffolding pole and laid into them indiscriminately.

The sheer ferocity and speed of his attack won him a precious second or two. The man he hit first took the blow on his head and went down as if poleaxed. A second man he hurled aside. The third hit him, but not hard enough. He delivered an elbow to the face and then took off, running hard, the adrenaline pumping. It had started.

CHAPTER NINETEEN

By now, under the *Reviving Homes* banner, the Taits had rebuilt, restored, refurbished and sold on upwards of a dozen houses and cottages. John did a lot of the work himself, bringing in local builders and tradesmen mostly for the big and the specialized stuff. The work gave him something to do and kept him fit, and he'd found that he liked it. The challenge of working with his hands gave him a sense of satisfaction he wouldn't have got from the office work alone. Sam — officially the in-house interior design consultant — enjoyed her role, too. Together, they were a good partnership, both at home and on site.

The profit from their work had given them their income, and their living. They had never decided what to do with the bulk of the money John had brought with him from Slovakia, but they hadn't needed it and they hadn't used it. One project funded the next, once a start had been made. And the profits had given them enough to live on. More important than financial considerations, though, the work had given them a life, a life enriched.

At present, they owned three properties they were working on. All were within a half hour's drive from home. One was an abandoned manse, another a ruined farmhouse and the third was a cottage in a neighbouring village.

The work was at different stages. The manse needed more negotiations with English Heritage before anything much could happen on site. The farmhouse had been a total ruin. Now it was rising again, like a barn conversion. That was where John had mostly been working of late. Sam had been focusing on the cottage, and the fixing and fitting, decorating and cleaning it needed.

Sam could have headed for any one of those three properties, when she left home without warning or preparation. She could have been reasonably assured that her husband would find them, and soon, if she and Kyle went to one of them.

But John's guess was that she had not opted for any of them. As well as being in their ownership, each of them was very accessible by road, too accessible. Much better, he could almost hear Sam thinking, to head for somewhere more remote, somewhere that no one would think to associate with them. No one but him, that is.

He was betting she had headed for Gimmer Hall, another ruin. It was a simple building in the hills, with a name that told of its ancient Scandinavian lineage, and there was no road to or anywhere near it. It was a long abandoned, tranquil place that they both liked. A couple of times they had picnicked there with Kyle, and once Sam had fantasized about it being a good place to escape the modern world. John had agreed with her.

If that really was where she and Kyle had headed, he knew they would need help soon in this weather. He even doubted they could actually reach it. What was it — five miles? That was a long trek over moorland at night in bad weather with a small child. Crazy even to try. So it was a risky bet, but he was putting all his money on it.

There was nowhere else that came to mind so readily, and he knew Sam. They had been through a lot together and understood each other well. Theirs was no ordinary relationship. It had been forged in fire, and tested. Contingency thinking, if not actual planning, had long been part of their life together.

If Gimmer Hall was where they had gone, Sam must have been truly desperate or terrified. Perhaps both. He had to get there fast. If they were not there, there wouldn't be much time left to search anywhere else for them — not if he was to find them still alive.

From the house he headed straight up on to the moor, moving fast despite the darkness and the weather. He knew this country, this patch of much-loved ground. It was his backyard, literally.

He hit the path he wanted and kept going hard, moving at a pace between a fast walk and a jog, neither the one nor the other, that once had been customary to him. It wasn't so easy now. He was older and long out of practice. But it was necessary. The incentive was greater than any he had ever known, and it drove him on relentlessly. He should reach Gimmer Hall in a couple of hours. There would be time then to rest.

As for the men behind him, they were the least of his worries. He wasn't even going to think about them, or who they were and what they wanted. Not now. He couldn't afford the distraction. If they followed him, he would divert and lose them. At night, in these conditions, and on this ground, he believed the odds were in his favour.

CHAPTER TWENTY

Sam knew someone was there. She had sensed it, seen the signs, for a day or two. Nothing terribly tangible. Just a hint, a suggestion. Once, she thought she saw movement in bushes above the house. Another time there was a brief flash of light on the hillside that reminded her of how guarded you needed to be when using field glasses surreptitiously.

Then there was a big four by four with darkened windows she didn't recognize. People around here didn't have that kind of vehicle, not one with darkened windows. They wanted to see and be seen. First, she saw it in the village a couple of times, and then it was on their own road, looking even more out of place.

Not much, but for someone with her background it began to add up, especially with John being away from home. Possible danger. Her old instincts came alive, putting her on guard, just as her father had advised she should always be. She wished John was here, but he wasn't. That was that. He wouldn't be back until tomorrow evening.

She didn't say anything when he phoned her, and she certainly didn't call him with her concerns. It would be silly to worry him about what might turn out to be nothing at all. She resolved to be careful, watchful. Maybe it really was nothing. Maybe her antennae would stop bristling. If that didn't happen, she would talk to him when he got home.

The next morning she woke up early and got herself and Kyle ready for school in good time. Before they left, she looked around the house and garden, looking for . . . well, for anything, really, anything out of the ordinary. There was nothing. The garage and the shed had not been broken into. Nothing had been stolen. There were no new footprints in soft earth, and no broken twigs near windows to suggest anyone had been prowling. Nothing at all that she could see.

Perhaps she was imagining it, she thought with relief, as they were about to leave for school. All the same, it was a long time, years even, since she had felt on edge this way. Life was so calm and settled here. They had nothing to worry about, and nothing had worried them. Why now? Why had it all started up again? The anxiety symptoms and the unease, the fear even. She didn't want all that to come back and take over her life once more.

Stop, she told herself firmly. Just stop — right now. Stop thinking and worrying about something that hasn't happened. Don't make a self-fulfilling prophecy out of it. Don't let it take you over. Divert yourself, woman!

She tried to put it all to one side, and concentrate on what Kyle was telling her about what they were going to do in school today. Making things, seemingly. Out of cardboard. That was why they had all been taking empty cereal boxes to school every day the past week.

'I'm doing a castle,' Kyle declared.

'A castle? Not a house, like Daddy builds?'

He shook his head. 'A castle's better. You can keep bad people out, with a castle.'

Just what we need, she thought. Just what I thought we had here. She corrected herself: what we do have here!

She smiled at her son, so earnest about his intentions. Where does that come from, she wondered? She hoped it wasn't from her, from what he'd seen in her the past day or two.

87

When John returned, she would make him laugh, telling him how jumpy she had been. He would just think she had missed him, and been lonely, which was true. She never had liked being apart from him. Since she came to England, separation had been a rare occurrence. They had made sure of that. But occasionally their business required it, as it had this time.

John had gone off for a few days to meet and discuss a possible project in the Scottish Borders, where a different legal system meant there were problems they didn't usually have in Northumberland. But he would be back soon, she thought with relief. This evening, in fact.

It wasn't exactly a busy day for her, but she did have things to do and people to see. As they were all in the village, she walked Kyle to school. It was a day when she could leave the car at home. In fact, she could leave everything at home. She had no need to return there either until she collected Kyle from school.

There was old Mrs Armstrong to visit, for a cup of tea and a chat. Then there was the man in the paper shop to see about getting in some special stationery. The bank manager wanted her to call him about something to do with their payments schedule. All little tasks and commitments, but they ate up the time and filled in her morning. Just after twelve she stopped by the cafe to grab a bowl of soup and to have a chat with her friend, Wendy, the owner.

In the afternoon, John called and told her he would be home in a couple of hours. Before she knew it, it was nearly time to collect Kyle. She gathered herself together and made tracks to the school.

By then, she had forgotten about her forebodings. But they all came back to her in an instant when she saw the unfamiliar four by four parked in a side street. Then she caught a glimpse of the passenger, sitting smoking with the window down.

She stopped, aghast. Yugov? Surely not? But it was. She was sure of it.

Shocked, terrified, she ducked her head and forced herself to hurry on, heart pounding, somehow resisting the temptation to stand and stare.

Her brain started working at feverish speed. Her focus was on Kyle. She needed to collect him and get him out of harm's way. Now!

Kyle wasn't the first child to appear through the school doorway, but he came soon enough. With only a brief smile and nod for other mothers, Sam took Kyle by the hand and led him away quickly.

She didn't take him the usual way, down the hill and through the village. She couldn't walk the gauntlet past that car, and risk discovering what Yugov wanted. She knew that anyway. She wasn't in any doubt.

Instead, she led a puzzled Kyle in the opposite direction, up a narrow footpath that led behind the school up on to the moor.

'Where are we going, Mummy?' Kyle protested.

'This way, for a change, darling,' she said.

She knew Kyle wasn't persuaded it was a good thing, but he didn't protest. Her only thought was the need to keep away from Yugov. Beyond that imperative, she couldn't think. She had no idea where they were going.

They couldn't go home. She knew that instinctively. There, they would be isolated and trapped. She couldn't involve anyone else, either, and risk endangering other people. On a practical level, there was no police presence in the village. So there was no possibility of asking them for help, even if she had been so inclined. And she had no phone with her to call John. She had nothing! They were on their own, she and Kyle.

She was still terrified, but her brain was working flat out. Even so, the only thing she knew for certain was that she had to keep herself and Kyle well away from Yugov.

Nothing else really mattered.

But where to go? What to do?

The light was fading. Soon it would be dark. It would be cold, too. She had to find some refuge for them both.

Where, though? It had to be somewhere John would think to look. It had to be a place where they would be safe until he found them, somewhere Yugov couldn't possibly know about. Where could they go? Where was there such a place?

As they toiled up the steep path, the answer suddenly came to her. There was one place no one else but John would think of. And he would! John would think of it. She was sure of it. He would find them there, and rescue them.

Then they would stand together and deal with Yugov. She couldn't fight him alone, not when she had Kyle to protect, but together with John she could. And, together, they would avenge her father.

CHAPTER TWENTY-ONE

Tait set a burning pace up the hillside and on to the moor. The way was steep and the night dark, and the rain was slanting into his face. None of that made any difference. He had to crack on. His wife and son were dependent on him finding them, and doing it soon. He had to rely on his strength and his knowledge of the hills to keep him ahead of the men on his trail while he searched for his family.

His thigh muscles were soon aching from the prolonged assault on the steep slope. His breath was coming in deep, lung-bursting gasps. Grimly, he forced himself on. He had to keep up the pace and try to burn off the pursuit.

Twice he paused, just for a moment, to listen. Each time he grimaced and set off again harder than ever. They were coming. He could hear them. Not voices. Just the rattle of loose stones slipping down the hillside.

He thought there were two, maybe three of them following. No more. They hadn't thought they would need more than that. They shouldn't have done, but he'd got his retaliation in first. Then he'd got lucky, and been able to get away.

They weren't far behind. He was hoping they would give it up, the chase, but they hadn't yet. On a night like this, that told him something about their capability, as well as their intentions. They were tough people, whoever they were.

He hoped to lose them when he reached the top and got out on to the moor. There was no single, well-trodden path up there. Just narrow sheep trails in all directions, in a sea of heather stretching for miles. He knew where he was going. They didn't.

It wouldn't be possible to see much up there on a night like this. Even here, on this broad, stony track, he couldn't really see where he was going. He was navigating more by memory, and the feel and sound of the ground underfoot, than vision.

The men following him couldn't know this country like he did, he kept telling himself. They were doing all right at the moment, but on the moor it would be a different story. Once he was up there, and off the path, he would be able to lose them and disappear.

He ducked his head to shield his eyes. Driven by a shrieking wind, the rain was heavier than ever now he was near the summit ridge. It was in his face, trickling down his collar and streaming down his back. There was nothing to be done about it. He couldn't stop. And if he pulled the hood of his jacket up, he would hear nothing.

The wetness didn't slow him down. He was more concerned by the many parts of his body that hadn't been tested like this for a long time and were complaining loudly. His thigh muscles were shrieking with pain. Threatening to go on strike. His lungs were raw with the harshness of his breathing.

He gritted his teeth and ignored it all. He ignored the pain in his back and legs. He ignored his bursting lungs. His focus was on reaching the top of the slope. His wife and son needed him. They needed him now — and alive.

Fifteen minutes after leaving the house, the gradient slackened off at last. He breasted the ridge and came up on to the open moor. Immediately, he shifted direction and turned hard to the north, leaving the track and taking a direct route through knee-high heather. There was no possibility of finding one of the sheep trails in this soggy, wet blackness. It didn't matter. He knew where he was going. Nobody behind him did.

Ten minutes later he paused to listen. Nothing at first. Then, in a lull in the wind, he heard a swishing sound. They were still there, brushing through the heather, and not far behind. He grimaced and changed direction again, heading westwards now.

Still the heather was high, but he knew he was close to grassland now. He would be able to move faster on that. But so would they, he thought with a grimace. That was no good.

He changed direction several times in his attempts to get rid of them. It made no difference. They were still there, and far too close. Closer, if anything. They were good, too good. Experienced hunters? Special Forces trained? He began to feel increasingly desperate. Whatever he did, he couldn't lose them.

How the hell were they doing it? They didn't know this country. They couldn't see any better than he could. And surely they couldn't hear him? It was uncanny.

Then it struck him. Either he was carrying a homing beacon they had managed to insert into him or his gear, which was virtually impossible, or they were using night-vision equipment. That was it! It had to be. Gear that used his own body heat to expose him.

Jesus! No wonder they were still there. They had a huge advantage. They hadn't been able to catch up with him yet, but they would wear him down eventually. He was one guy; they could swap pacemakers. What the hell could he do?

He'd better come up with something soon. Charging across the moor like this was not helping. He had to find some way of breaking things up, and causing confusion and uncertainty. He had to get far enough away from them that they lost all trace of him.

He thought fast. His mental map was good. He knew almost exactly where he was. He saw a possibility. About a quarter mile to the north there was a sandstone escarpment,

Friar's Edge. If he could reach that, something might be possible. He knew how to get down it fast. They didn't. It might make enough of a difference.

He reached the scarp edge. It was a half mile long, a thirty-foot-high tangle of sheer faces and huge boulders. Great fun to explore and climb around on a warm, dry summer's day. Impossible on a black, wet night this time of year — unless you knew your way around.

He headed straight for a gully he remembered. Without hesitation, he slithered down it fast, ignoring the bumps and scrapes. This was one place where the scree was only gravel. There were no rocks and boulders to break your leg, or your neck.

He reached the bottom of the gully without crippling himself. Just scrapes and knocks to knees and elbows, and once a hard jolt to his back. He scrambled back to his feet and set off to jog down a long slope of rough grassland, desperate to get out of the range of whatever equipment they were using.

They hadn't been close enough to see exactly what he'd done, and even if they had head lamps, they would struggle to find a quick way down the escarpment. The next few minutes were absolutely crucial. He had to get away from them now, or he never would.

Ten minutes later he stopped running. For a moment, he stooped and doubled over to catch his breath and to listen. Then he was off again, heading south now. He hadn't heard anything behind him for a while, and he was beginning to dare to hope he'd lost them.

Now he had to press on to Gimmer Hall. He had to get to Sam and Kyle before anyone else, or hypothermia, did.

CHAPTER TWENTY-TWO

It was a poor afternoon, threatening to turn into a bad night. Cloud was low on the hills and rain was blowing in from the west on a stiffening wind. She wondered if they could manage, but knew they would have to manage. There really wasn't any choice.

She knew what Yugov had done to her father, and to his colleagues and friends. Now he had come for her, and for her son. She was under no illusions. The past ten years had made her soft and delusional. But evil had not left the world. Now had come the day of reckoning.

'Mummy!' Kyle wailed. 'I'm cold and my tummy hurts.'

'I know, darling. But we must keep going. Trust me. Some bad men have come looking for us. We must get out of their way, and wait for Daddy.'

'Bad men? I didn't see them.'

'They were there, in a big black car. I saw them.'

She said no more. She didn't want to terrify him altogether. They ploughed on, climbing the steep, muddy slope in poor light, with wind and rain in their faces.

Kyle was soon suffering but she couldn't give into his entreaties. She couldn't carry him, either. He was too heavy. So she had to require him to keep walking.

How far was it? Ten kilometres? Something like that. Not a vast distance. They could do that, walk that far. However bad it got, they would manage. They must.

She wondered why Yugov had turned up here now, after all these years. How did he know they were here, and why come now? What did he want? Had he come for the money, the money that John had brought from Slovakia?

She shook her head. It seemed unlikely. After all this time? How did he even know they had it? And, again, how did he know where to come? No. It must be another reason.

Then something else dawned on her. Was it possible? She shook her head again. How could he know what her father had told her? It simply wasn't possible. Surely not? But he might . . . Forget it, she told herself angrily. It doesn't matter. He's here. That's all that counts.

And it was. She knew that. Yugov was here, and she had to evade him. If she couldn't, she would find out soon enough what he wanted. They all would.

Rain began to fall more heavily, and with it came a strong, gusting wind. If the hillside had been bad enough, the moor itself was atrocious. They battled on in the teeth of a gathering storm but she began to realize it was a losing battle they were fighting. They weren't going to make it. It was too far in these conditions. To make matters worse, daylight was almost gone now. Their future seemed to be fading with it.

It was then that she realized she hadn't heard Kyle for a few minutes. She stopped and leant down to kiss his face and tell him they had to go on a little further.

It was no use. His eyes were closed. His face was wet and cold. He couldn't hear her. He was spent. Desperately, she wrapped her arms around him and hugged him hard. It was no. He was asleep on his feet, and very cold. She knew they had to find shelter. They had to find it now, before it was too late.

CHAPTER TWENTY-THREE

At last! He stumbled up to the stone wall that surrounded Gimmer Hall. Getting here had taken the best part of four hours, counting the diversions he had had to make. The wall was in a state of collapse along its entire length, but it was still an imposing piece of masonry. He picked his way over it in one of the lower sections, taking care on the greasy stones. It was no time to risk spraining an ankle, or worse.

'Sam!' he called as he approached the ruined building. 'It's me. Are you there, Sam? Sam, Kyle?'

He waited, the tension almost unbearable, but all he heard was the sound of rainwater dripping somewhere. With a grimace, he took out a small torch from his rucksack. He didn't switch it on yet. Instead, he called softly again. Still no answer.

Using his hand to shade the torch and create a thin beam of light, he made his way through what had once been a doorway and clambered inside. The torch revealed an open space cluttered with heaps of rubble. The internal walls of the house had long since disappeared, and he could see the entire interior of the building. There was no one here now, and he could see no signs of anyone having been here recently.

So they hadn't come here, after all. His head dropped and he sagged against a wall, worn out by the emptiness he had found, along with everything that had happened in the past few hours. He switched the torch off and stood motionless, trying to cope with the disappointment, and with the knowledge that his frantic journey had wasted time and effort. They weren't here.

The thinking process began to kick in again after a couple of minutes. He straightened up, mentally and physically. They were somewhere else, obviously. The Russians, or whatever the hell they were, still hadn't got them. That was the good news. Not exactly news, perhaps, but definitely good. Something to cling to.

They were still out there somewhere. Where, though? Where else might Sam have gone? He had no idea. Couldn't even begin to guess. Gimmer Hall had been his banker.

He soon concluded that he ought to get back home fast. Maybe they would turn up there, after all. It was stupid of him to have imagined they would trek all this way, in the night, and in this weather. They couldn't have done it. It had been bad enough for him. For them, it would have been impossible.

He glanced at his watch. Gone four now. In another three hours there would be some daylight. He could be back home by then. He'd better go — and be ready for whatever he found there. Maybe a deal could be done with these people. It seemed unlikely, but he had to think positively. While there was breath in his body, he would fight and trade and scheme. It was his family he was searching for, and trying to protect. He would do what it took to keep them safe.

The return journey was hard going. No one was chasing him now. So there was no adrenaline pulsing through his body to hide the pain and protect against fear, and to force more effort from weary limbs. There was nothing to help make light of the journey. He just had to endure the dull plodge through a wet, muddy landscape in the dark, with all the fear and dread that on the way out he hadn't had time to think about. He was tired, too, and cold. His body ached from careening around the moor for several hours in the dark and the rain, and it was hard to stave off the growing fatigue.

Just press on, he urged himself. Straighten up! Get back there and fight. You've been in bad places, and bad times before. Nothing new about it.

Fight what, though? Fight who? Russian or Ukrainian gangsters? That was probably what they were. One or the other. He didn't know now, but would find out for sure eventually.

It was time to call in some help. If he didn't find Sam and Kyle at home, which he didn't expect, he would do that. To hell with the consequences. He couldn't fight this on his own.

By six it was still black night, but as the hour neared seven, light began to edge its way across the moor to reveal an eerie landscape. The rain had ceased at last, the relentless, driving rain with a westerly wind behind it. Now the land was cloaked in isolated banks of hill fog and a fine drizzle that soaked any small part of him that had somehow managed to stay dry.

A myriad spider webs glistened across the surface of the heather, where tiny droplets of moisture from the drizzle and mist were caught in their clutches. He stumbled over a pair of grouse sheltering in the undergrowth. They took off belatedly, reluctantly, croaking raucously as with heavy beating of their wings, they attempted lift-off for the first time that morning. I know just how you feel, he thought ruefully. None of us is up to much after a night like that. He tried not to speculate on how his wife and son would be.

His legs were made of rubber. His back ached more than it would have done if he had unloaded a lorry load of bricks by hand. But with the growing light, fresh reserves of energy began to stir, fed by renewed determination and fear. There was so much he needed to do.

He stopped dead, hearing a strange sound, one that was out of place. He stopped walking, stood still and concentrated hard. Nothing. He couldn't hear it now.

What the hell was it? An odd noise to hear out here. Something almost human about it. A voice, perhaps? No, not that. More likely a trick of the atmospheric conditions and his own fatigue.

He turned and looked around. Nothing. There was nothing to be seen, or to be heard now, either. He shrugged. His ears playing tricks on him. If it wasn't his eyes, it was his ears. He was in a sad state.

He knew where he was, though. Familiar territory. He hadn't far to go. Close by was a narrow path he might well have used last night if he'd been able to see it. Even the half-light of the pre-dawn was a wonderful thing when you were used to having your head stuck in a black velvet bag.

There! Again. That sound that had stopped him in his tracks.

He froze for a moment. Then he looked around and made for a particularly thick clump of high heather. He reached down to part the heather.

Oh God, no!

Two bodies: one big, one small.

It was them. He reached for them desperately.

CHAPTER TWENTY-FOUR

Sam's eyes opened and she looked up at him. She stared, dazed and uncomprehending. He reached down to feel her face. Cold. She was cold, but she was awake.

'Come on, sweetheart!' he said urgently. 'Let's get you moving.'

He stooped to kiss her face, and then turned his attention to Kyle. The boy seemed to be sleeping. His pulse was strong, though. Thank God!

'John?' Sam muttered. 'You found us.'

'Of course I did! You knew I would, didn't you?'

'Yes. It's been so cold, John. I didn't know what to do.'

'You did well, very well. Stopping here, in shelter, was the best thing you could have done.'

He slipped the rucksack off his back and opened it up. He pulled out gloves and a woollen hat, and handed them to her. 'Come on, now! Get these on. And here's a chocolate bar. Eat it.'

Kyle was stirring, too, now. He fitted a hat on the boy. Then he picked him up, and hugged and kissed him, murmuring to him all the while. When Kyle's eyes opened, he smiled at him and kissed him again.

'Daddy?' Kyle said plaintively.

'It is! I've come to find you. Come on, son! Here's some chocolate for you.'

'Cold,' Kyle whispered. 'I'm cold.'

'I know you are. But don't worry. We'll get moving, and warm you up again.'

The boy was shivering, shaking, which wasn't such a bad thing. Better, at least, than if the shivering phase had stopped. Sam was shivering, too. They were both very cold and exhausted. It was worrying. What to do for the best?

Getting them both home from here would take a couple of hours, at least. Too long, and probably too far for him to carry Kyle anyway.

He thought fast as he pulled out gloves and more chocolate from his rucksack. Another possibility came to mind. Only half the distance. He could get them there. But he was going to have to get Sam back on her feet first. No point being soft about it. He couldn't carry them both.

'Come on, Sam!' he said brusquely, sternly. 'On your feet. We've got to get moving.'

It was hard going, even though the rain and wind had abated now. The ground was sodden, with black pools of filthy bog water interspersed amongst the knee-high heather. Progress was slow. They splashed on, saturated, worn down by fatigue and cold. No matter how tired and sore they were, he knew they had to keep moving while they still could.

Fortunately, Sam wanted to talk now she was half-awake. That helped.

'I didn't know what to do,' she said. 'I panicked when I saw Yugov.'

'Yugov?' John repeated, aghast. 'Is it him?'

She nodded. 'All I knew was that I had to collect Kyle from school, and get out of their way.'

'I understand. You did well. But save it for now,' he told her, Kyle heavy in his arms. 'Wait until we're somewhere warm and safe. Then we'll talk.'

'Where are we going, John? This isn't the way home, is it?'

'No, it isn't. You're right. We're heading over to the next valley. It's nearer, and there's a place there we can use.'

'Kyle . . .' she began.

'Kyle's fine! Aren't you, young man?'

He smiled down at the boy, and was relieved to see a glimmer come back from him. They were both better than they had any right to be, he thought. They were shivering and exhausted — hypothermia was still a real risk — but Sam had done a good job in sheltering Kyle and keeping them both alive.

As for why she had run in the first place, further explanation could wait. Yugov, though! A nightmare come true. He couldn't believe it. But Sam wouldn't be making that up. She wouldn't be mistaken either.

'All right, love?' he asked, turning to her with an encouraging smile.

She gave him a wan smile back. 'All right,' she whispered.

'Another twenty minutes,' he said. 'That's all. Can you keep going that long?'

'Do you doubt it?' she responded more briskly, rising to the challenge.

He laughed. His family. He was proud of them.

With arms aching and growing numb from carrying Kyle, he led the way off the moor and down the hillside into the next little valley. He was heading for a building that was enclosed on three sides by a shelter belt of scots pine.

Sam stumbled and fell into him from behind.

'Steady!' he said, gently holding on to her for a moment. 'Nearly there now,' he added softly.

She was exhausted. He could see that. They all were, but Sam most of all. And he couldn't carry her as well as Kyle.

'Is that where we're we going?' she asked wearily. 'That building? What is it?'

It looked like an old stone farmhouse, which was what it had been until the Ministry of Defence had claimed it, as part of their estate, and put it into occasional use as accommodation for troops on training exercises and manoeuvres.

'We're right on the edge of the Otterburn Ranges here,' he said. 'That's one of the MOD buildings.'

'What's it for?'

'Soldiers — the British Army — when they have exercises. We'll stop there and rest. Get warmed up, as well,' he added with a grin.

She didn't bother responding. Her head went down and she got back to putting one foot in front of the other.

Fifteen minutes later, they approached the farmhouse that was no longer the centre of a working farm. There were other houses like it in nearby valleys, MOD properties now, all of them. In some cases, the farms were operated in the traditional way by tenant farmers. In others, like this one, the land was worked still, or grazed rather, by neighbouring farms, but the houses and outbuildings had not been lived in by farm folk for a long time.

John stood still on the faint path through the heather he had picked up and studied what he could see of the buildings ahead of him. No lights. Pretty dark still, especially down in the valley, but no lights showing. No smoke in the air that he could detect, either. No vehicles standing outside. No sound of a generator. Nothing. Almost certainly empty, as these places were a lot of the time.

He glanced up at the sky. Under a thick cloud, a heavy drizzle had started up again. All three of them were sodden and ice-cold already, and this wouldn't help. But he forced himself to think objectively before they moved on, and did something he might have cause to regret later. What were the options?

He soon came to the conclusion that they didn't really have an option worth thinking about. To survive, and recover, they had to break into the farmhouse. There was nothing else they could do.

'John?' Sam said tentatively. 'Is it safe?'

He nodded. 'I think so. Come on!' he added briskly. 'Let's get on with it.'

Entry proved easy. Out in the wilds, even the MOD seemed pretty relaxed about security. A padlock and a sign warning against entry by unauthorized persons seemed to cover it.

John got in through a window with a loose pane of glass that he carefully removed. Then Sam handed Kyle to him, and climbed through herself. He propped the loose glass back in place.

'Dark,' Sam said, sniffing suspiciously.

'There can be no lights without the generator going, and we're not going to risk that,' he told her. 'At least it's dry in here.'

They were in the main room on the ground floor. It served as a kitchen and general activity area. There was a Calor gas stove for cooking, a wood-burning stove for heating, and a dozen dining chairs set around a big table. Not much else. Not much else would be needed, John thought. Just somewhere to sleep, which would be upstairs, probably bunk-house style. A quick inspection confirmed that.

Not surprisingly, the house was in pretty good shape, he decided. The MOD knew how to look after its property. A lot of men could be accommodated here at the drop of a hat, and in more comfort — not to mention safety — than they would experience in the likes of Afghanistan and Iraq.

A bunch of keys hanging over the kitchen sink allowed him to unlock the front door. After that, he checked the main outhouse, a converted barn, and found it much the same as the house. He noted the bunk beds and cooking stove, the storage lockers and tool chests, the tables and bench seats. You couldn't fault the MOD, he thought with satisfaction.

'I'm not going to risk lighting a fire,' he told Sam when he returned, thinking of the men who had pursued him so relentlessly. 'The smell of the smoke might give us away. But we can heat some water for hot drinks. While I connect a gas canister, can you look around to see if there's anything else we can use?'

It was a simple matter to get the gas stove working. By the time he'd done that, and put on a kettle of water, Sam was back with some sleeping bags she had found upstairs.

'There are bunk beds upstairs,' she said.

He nodded. 'Better to stay together down here for now, though.'

They took off their wet coats and hung them up to drip. Then they got Kyle into one sleeping bag, and Sam into another. By then, the water in the kettle was hot enough for John to make hot chocolate from sachets he had brought with him.

'Mm!' Sam said with contentment, despite her chattering teeth. 'Hot chocolate! My favourite.'

'I like it, too, Daddy!' said a revitalized Kyle.

'Of course you do,' John said with a big grin. 'That's why I brought it.'

He took mugs from the collection hanging on hooks near the cooker and poured drinks for them all. Then he pulled a chair across to where they had laid out the sleeping bags.

'You and Kyle can get some sleep, Sam, but first tell me briefly what happened.'

He listened intently as Sam retraced their steps, and the course of their day. There wasn't a lot to tell, in truth, but it wasn't hard to see why she had grabbed Kyle from school and fled. Nowhere had seemed safe.

'Yugov, eh?' he said afterwards, shaking his head. He didn't ask her if she was sure.

There was no need.

'I panicked, John. All I knew was that we had to get away. I daren't go back home.'

He nodded. 'That wasn't panic. It was common sense. You did the right thing. Did you head for Gimmer Hall?'

'Yes. I believed you would find us there.'

He smiled ruefully. 'I guessed as much, and was very disappointed not to find you there.'

'We couldn't go any further,' she said sadly. 'Kyle was so cold and tired. I wasn't much better myself, and I couldn't carry him.'

He nodded. He didn't want her to recall all that. It was too recent, and too raw an experience.

'What about you?' Sam asked.

'You weren't home when I got back. Then I received a phone call.' He shrugged and added, 'I didn't know then exactly who it was, but I had a good idea. They just said they were here, they had come.'

'For the money?'

He shrugged. 'I suppose so, but they didn't say. Why now, though, after all this time? And how did they find us?'

'They have ways,' Sam said with a sigh.

'Not very efficient ways. We've been here a long time. If I can talk to them, I'll give them the money gladly. It's no use to us anyway.'

'I believe they are not here for that reason,' she said.

'Not for the money?'

She shook her head.

'Then why have they come?'

'For me,' she said bleakly. 'They want me.'

CHAPTER TWENTY-FIVE

Riley soon became frustrated. He couldn't live with the pace these guys were setting. I'm too old for this, he decided. They're going to fucking kill me!

By then, he had climbed the hillside and reached the edge of the moor but there was no one in sight or earshot anymore. They'd all vanished into the sea of darkness that blanketed the moor.

He couldn't understand how the hell they'd managed it. Tait knew the country hereabouts, but the guys going after him — Yugov's people — certainly didn't. Still, there it was. They were gone, the whole damned lot of them.

He paused for a breather, and a bit of reflection. His money was on Tait staying ahead of them, at least for a while. He was on home ground. Also, he had a lot of incentive. In the long run, though, it would be a different matter. He wasn't so sure about the eventual outcome.

But why had Tait suddenly upped and run? Was it just to get away from the people coming for him? Was it to collect the Olsson money before they got to it? Or was it for some other reason?

And what had happened to Tait's wife and kid? He hadn't seen them all day, and that was nagging away at him.

If they'd been abducted, where were they? And what was Tait doing? Was he abandoning them to save his own skin?

Then there was Comrade Yugov's friends. What the hell were they doing in this godforsaken little place in the back of nowhere? If Yugov had joined the dotted lines and connected everything to Tait, why not until now? Why had it taken him ten years?

Why, also, had all this happened at the same time as Ted Pearson had reactivated him? Hard to believe that was just a coincidence. Surely not?

Besides, how had Yugov known where to find Tait? The same way as Ted Pearson had? Had he independently followed the same evidence trail? Or had he been tipped off? Had Washington sprung yet another leak?

So many questions. He shook his head. It was beyond him.

Dropping down from the skyline, to shelter from the driving rain, he rested a few moments while he considered what to do next. Part of him felt like just walking away, and letting Yugov's people get on with it. That didn't seem such a bad idea. No need for him to be there for the kill.

Admittedly, he was here to see that Tait was taken down, but it wouldn't matter to him, or to Ted Pearson probably, if someone else pulled the trigger. It would just save him a lot of hard work on this bitch of a night.

On the other hand, he mused, it would also leave the circumstances of Jack Olsson's death a mystery still. He really would like to know more about what had happened back then. And so would Ted, he guessed.

The appearance of Yugov's henchman, Kuznetsov, and his buddies was something else that needed explaining. He would like to know about that, too. And he wouldn't be the only one. Yugov was a person of perpetual interest to all the intelligence agencies back in DC.

So, all things considered, he'd better stay a while, and try to find answers to some of those questions.

By then, he had given up on the hot chase. Instead, he came down the hill and headed back to his car, which was parked out of the way at the end of the Taits' road. Then he got his head down for a couple of hours.

He didn't want to spend time returning to the hotel. At first light he wanted to be up on that darned moor, to see what he could find. It might well be a lifeless body, but you never could tell. Tait might prove to be smarter than he looked. He would need to be good, though, to escape from Yugov's men. They were tough, resourceful people. He knew that from past experience.

He shook his head and closed his eyes. This situation was like Churchill's old description of Russia: an enigma wrapped up in a riddle.

Just after six he woke up. He spent a few minutes sipping from a flask of coffee while he ate a ham sandwich, both of which he had with great foresight stored in the car. He wasn't hungry, but he knew, as an old field hand, that you needed to take sustenance on board when you could.

By the time he was done, the blackness all around was starting to fade a little. If he started off now, there should be enough grey light by seven to see his way across the moor. Better make a start.

He followed the broad track back up the hillside easily enough in the near dark. On top, he rested a few minutes and watched a little more light seep in from the east. Already he knew there were plenty of narrow paths, sheep trails mostly, across the moor, but he waited until he could see footprints in the mud before he set off after Tait and his trackers.

There was plenty to follow. Footprints from a few hours earlier. They had all been in a hurry. Nobody had bothered trying to conceal their tracks. He picked them up easily and followed them through the wet heather and the swampy bits in between, where rain water had puddled and failed to drain.

Although the light was perceptibly increasing, visibility was not great. The heavy rain had stopped, but cloud hung low on the moor and there were patches of hill fog and sudden flurries of drizzle to dampen things down and impede progress.

He couldn't see very far ahead but that didn't matter, so long as he didn't run into anyone with hostile intent. All he really needed right now was just a bit more light, so he could follow the new tracks more easily.

Soon, though, the tracks became confusing. They changed direction frequently, and spread out and closed back in again. He puzzled over them initially. Three or four guys had come this way. One of them was Tait himself. So the others were trying to keep up with him. How the hell had they done that in the dark and the heavy rain?

Then he nodded. He'd got it. The only way was if they were using night-vision equipment. Some state-of-the-art gear.

Even so, they had struggled at times. The evidence was there on the ground. Tait had kept changing course, almost at random, and when he did that the guys following him separated, to make sure they didn't miss him. Once one of them had him back in sight, they closed up again.

Tait didn't have gear like that. Riley nodded again, this time with grudging approval and respect. The man had set a cracking pace and used his wits to the full. To be able to keep ahead of men who had to be military trained, and military fit, said quite a lot about him. In fact, the whole damned lot of them were like Special Forces people, Tait included. He wondered just how long the fox had been able to stay ahead of the hounds.

Things changed when the chase came to a rocky escarpment. With the eye of an expert hunter, Riley interpreted the marks on the ground and saw what had happened. Tait had been struggling to get clean away and had brought them to this place deliberately, figuring he would have a better chance here than on the open moor.

If he could only get ahead by a few minutes, he would have thought, they would lose sight of him despite their fancy gear. Then he could take off in a straight line and get the hell away. Was that what had happened?

111

It looked like it. Tait had made home advantage count. Riley found the spot where one man had slithered down a gully and out across a sandy stretch at the bottom. Other tracks showed that his followers had missed the gully and had hunted along the crest of the ridge, looking for a way down that wasn't a suicidal leap into the dark. They had found it at the end of the escarpment. But by then it had been too late. Tait had won the valuable time and distance he needed, and had been able to get clear.

Riley stood on a slab of bare sandstone and stared out into the growing dawn light. So Tait had done it, he thought with grudging respect. From a standing start, he had bested the four hard men who had come for him and got clean away. For now. But could he keep it up?

CHAPTER TWENTY-SIX

John decided to let Sam sleep until she woke up herself. Kyle, too. As for himself, he was certainly tired, exhausted even — it had been a long time since he had last had a night like that — but the adrenaline was racing around his system still and would keep him awake as long as necessary.

There was a lot on his mind. Relief, of course, that he had found Sam and Kyle, and found them no worse than wet, cold and tired. More pressing now, though, was how they were going to get out of here, and where they were going to go.

Simply going home seemed out of the question. Somehow they had to get help, which probably meant they had to find a way of contacting the police and persuading them of the threat they were under. Explaining a lot of things, too. Such as Sam's illegal status. And why anyone in the world — particularly Russian terrorists, or an organized crime gang from eastern Europe — should be after them.

Then what? What would happen after that? He had no idea. He just knew it wouldn't be easy.

Miss out the police, then? Contact someone else? But who? Some young kid on the MI5 or MI6 helpline?

Basically, he had no idea who to contact. Besides, official involvement would probably spell the end of everything he and Sam had worked for here. But what else could they do?

Anyway, even doing that was easier said than done. They had to get off the moor first. Yugov's people were still out there, and their objectives wouldn't have changed. They would want the money, all $10,000,000 worth of it — and probably him dead, as well. Probably Sam, too. Or Vlasta, as they would still call her.

That brought him back to Sam's belief that it was her they were after, not the money he had brought from Slovakia all those years ago. What on earth made her think that? Surely it couldn't just be a matter of wiping out the last remnant of Viktor Sirko's family? Did their relentlessness run that deep? After all this time?

He shook his head. He had no idea. For now, anyway, he had more pressing matters to consider. Short-term matters. If things went badly, the short term would be all the time they had.

He made his way around the building. It didn't take him long. This had been a very simple farmhouse, like so many others in the hills. Originally, there had been one large room downstairs that served as a kitchen and living room, plus a back scullery and cupboards. Upstairs there had been two bedrooms. That had been it. No bathroom. No inside toilet. Not even running water. All that had been dealt with outdoors.

Now, after the MOD conversion, the building had one big room downstairs still, and another, a dormitory, upstairs. A bathroom extension had been built, and there was piped water to that and to the kitchen. The house had a front and a back door, and windows on three sides. The one side that was windowless was close up against the steep hillside.

He stood to one side of the main window in the downstairs room and frowned thoughtfully. They were in the process of drying off and warming up here, and they had needed somewhere to rest, but they would have to hope Yugov's men didn't find them. The house was indefensible. He couldn't hope to hold off several attackers for long with his one hand gun.

'John!' Sam called softly.

He turned with a smile to meet her.

'John, you need some rest, too. You lie down for a while. I'll keep watch.'

He didn't argue with her. He knew she was right. Exhaustion could lead to bad decisions and big mistakes. Even an hour's sleep would be a big help.

'What about Kyle?' he asked.

'He's all right.' Sam put a hand to her mouth to stifle a yawn, and apologized for it. 'I don't think he will wake up soon.'

He nodded and made for the sleeping bag she had left. They were lucky to have it, he thought as he surrendered to the fatigue that had been threatening to overcome him for some time.

He was up again in a couple of hours. By then, it was late morning. The weather hadn't changed. It looked like being another of those days when the world is liquid, and the difference between earth and sky is academic.

'Anything happening?' he asked, getting out of the sleeping bag.

Sam shook her head.

'Good. How's Kyle?'

'He's fine, I think. Just very tired still. He woke up, but soon went back to sleep again.'

That was good, he thought. The little fella needed some rest. He'd probably wake up with a raging appetite too.

'John, what are we going to do?'

'Stay here for a little while, I think. We need to talk. After that, we'll decide our next step.'

'Talk?' she said with a sigh. 'Is that all we can do?'

'At the moment, yes. But we can eat first. I brought some packets of dried food. Let's see what we can do with them.'

He delved into his rucksack and hauled out various packages. All of them contained dried foods that could be reconstituted and made ready to eat by adding water and heating them up.

'I didn't know we had all this,' Sam said with surprise.

'It's so long since I used any of it, I'd almost forgotten myself.'

They heated up some stew and ate it avidly. Hunger improved the taste. Coffee followed.

'What do you think is going on?' John asked then. 'Why has Yugov suddenly appeared on the scene?'

Sam shrugged. 'Who knows? Information has become available, perhaps.'

'After all this time?' he asked sceptically. 'Where from?'

'People like him are always on the alert. They spend their lives scheming and planning, taking advantage of opportunities.'

'Like Viktor?'

'Yes, in a way.' She sighed and added, 'But my father did only legal things.'

'Of course,' John said with an ironic smile. 'Always.'

'Well, perhaps not absolutely all of the time, but mostly. He was very different to Yugov, though. Yugov was always a vicious criminal, from the very beginning. Father didn't mind competition in business, but Yugov . . . well, he was always different.'

'I'll grant you that. I saw some of that in action. Is he Russian?'

'Well . . . Ukrainian, I think, but one of the Russian-speaking Ukrainians from the east. Father thought he was far enough away from Donetsk to be safe, but he wasn't, was he?'

John shook his head. That much was certainly true.

'Sam, what did you mean when you said you thought they had come here for you?'

'Oh, nothing,' she said with a sigh. 'I don't know what I meant. It was just talk, that's all.'

He frowned. He wasn't satisfied, but he didn't want to press her.

'Yugov must be here for the money,' he reasoned. 'Somehow he found out I took it. Somehow. But how — ten years later?'

'I don't know, John. Does it really matter anyway? It's more important to talk about what we should do now.'

He was saved from answering by Kyle waking up with a little cry. Sam rushed to comfort him. When he was properly awake, she fed him some of the stew. He wrinkled his nose and grimaced, but he ate a little.

He must be hungry, John thought with a wry smile. Then he returned to the question Sam had asked. The truth was that getting out of here without being intercepted was going to be a problem, one he had little idea how to solve.

They would wait a little longer, he decided. Let their clothing dry some more. See if the weather changed. Do a bit more thinking, and try to work out a feasible plan.

After eating, Kyle was better, less tired, more like himself. He began playing. He explored the old house. John went upstairs with him to look around the dormitory.

'Soldiers stay here sometimes,' he explained to his wide-eyed son. 'They sleep here.'

'Real ones?'

'Real ones.'

That aroused Kyle's imagination. Further exploration and explanation necessarily took place. Father and son enjoyed a happy half hour.

Then things changed.

'John!' Sam called urgently from downstairs. 'We have company.'

He darted to the window and glanced out across the valley. Then he grimaced and swore softly. It was what he had feared and dreaded might happen.

CHAPTER TWENTY-SEVEN

They lost him on the escarpment, and they couldn't track in the dark once they no longer had a thermal image. So they stayed where they were, and waited. They waited for daybreak.

Three, maybe four hours it would be, Kuznetsov said. The others nodded and settled down to make the best of it. They could do that. They were men with a lot of experience of mountain battlefields. This hill country was easy for them after the North Caucasus.

Kuznetsov phoned Yugov on his sat phone.

'Well, you know what to do,' Yugov said. 'I must return now. Things are happening. Do what you have to do, and then get out of there. Come back to join me as soon as you can.'

Kuznetsov said they would. Then he switched off and settled down like the others to an impromptu bivouac amongst the rocks at the foot of the escarpment. They were out of the wind and much of the rain. They could wait for daylight. Their quarry would not escape. They were used to pursuit, and used to killing. They had been doing it for a long time. This chase would end like all the others.

As the light started to spread over the land they began to stir. They had neither food nor drink with them, but it was of no concern. They were accustomed to that. They were used to eating and drinking when they could, and to doing without when they could not. It made little difference to them, or to their effectiveness. They were from a hard school.

In growing light they spread out along the foot of the escarpment, looking for tracks. It was Yudin who found them. He studied them for a few moments. Then he signalled the others with a sharp whistle. They gathered together, spoke briefly and then set off to see where the tracks led.

Tait had done his best to avoid leaving footprints. Mostly he had trod on heather and grass, and left little trace. Just occasionally he had left a boot mark in mud. It was easy to follow his progress, although sometimes it was slow going.

After a couple of hours they neared a ruined building. Kuznetsov called a halt. He studied the building carefully before making a cautious approach. It was a waste of time. There was no one there.

'Maybe he met the woman here?' Volkov suggested. 'The woman and the boy?'

'Maybe,' Kuznetsov said, shaking his head as if to say it was unlikely. 'No footprints. Could the woman and the boy have got here anyway, on their own?'

No one replied. No one knew the answer to that question, but they all knew it was unlikely.

Kuznetsov looked around the interior of the ruined building for a few minutes. Then he skirted the outside, eyes glued to the ground.

'There was no one here,' he announced finally. 'He came here, I think, possibly expecting to meet someone — the woman and the boy, perhaps, as you suggested, Volkov — but they were not here. So then he turned round and left. I can find only his footprints. They come here, and then they go away again.'

'So where are they?' Yudin asked.

Kuznetsov shrugged.

'Maybe they went back to the house?' Volkov suggested.

'I think not,' Kuznetsov said. 'But I will call Belkin to make sure.'

'If he's woken up yet!' Yudin sniggered.

Kuznetsov smiled his agreement. 'He's getting soft, old Belkin. Letting a man like this hit him so hard? He should remember his army training. Remember Chechnya. We all should. Maybe we're all getting soft. No more though,' he added with a gleam in his eye. 'We are close now. We will soon have what we need.'

We had better, he thought. Yugov was never patient with failure.

They spread out again and returned to tracking their prey. It wasn't so easy now. Tait had set off on his new journey along a much-travelled, compacted, stony track. They needed to know whether he had stayed on that track or diverted at some point and taken yet another path.

Eventually, they were standing on the ridge overlooking the Taits' house again. Yudin ran down the hill to check the house. He found no one there. Not even Belkin, he reported when he returned.

Kuznetsov weighed it up, and decided Belkin had probably recovered and gone to the airport to join Yugov. Otherwise, he would still be where they had left him, or nearby. The important point was that Tait had not returned. Nor had the woman and the boy.

'We will search again, and find these people,' he told the others. 'Yugov expects us to get what he needs from them.'

They knew that. They hadn't really needed to be told.

So they spread out once more and began to quarter the moor systematically, in daylight now, gradually spreading further and further afield.

It was Yudin who, several hours later, spotted a building in a nearby valley. He studied it for a few minutes. There was no sign of life there. Probably abandoned, he decided. To make sure, he began to descend the hillside.

Halfway down he came across a wide patch of muddy ground, just below a spring where water bubbled to the surface. That was where he saw recent tracks, a lot of them. People had come this way, and not long ago.

He stared down at the old house again and nodded. It made sense. They must be there. They had to be. Nobody else would have come this way in the last few hours, and there was nowhere else for them to be. He pulled out his phone and called Kuznetsov.

CHAPTER TWENTY-EIGHT

He saw what Sam meant. A man was approaching the front of the house. Tough looking and vigilant, he came forward purposefully. He knows we're here, he thought. If he's one of Yugov's men from last night, he won't be alone either.

He motioned Sam to collect Kyle and move aside. Then he opened the front door and stood facing the visitor. The man stopped, about ten yards away.

'Tait?'

John nodded.

'I want to talk to your woman,' the newcomer said in a gruff voice.

Not English, obviously. Heavy accent.

'My wife, you mean? What about?'

'The message is for her ears alone.'

Good English, but possibly a Russian speaker.

'You can tell me.'

'Only your wife. Don't make this more difficult than it already is.'

'It's not going to happen, pal. I suggest you clear off. Who are you anyway?'

'We have no time to waste. I want you to know that before anything else happens.'

John shook his head. 'Like I said, no way. Now piss off.'

Then two other figures came into view, one from each side of the house. The three of them spoke together in Russian. John understood parts of it. He understood that the main one wanted to know if the woman was here, and one of the others said he'd seen her through the window.

Damn! They didn't have a leg to stand on now, John thought desperately. They knew who was inside the house.

The main man turned back to him. 'One last time. We will speak to your woman, whether you want us to or not. Yes?'

John stood his ground and shook his head. 'Anything you want to say, you can say to me.'

Two of them came for him then, one from each side. Strong men, trained fighters. The doorway was no place to take them on, but it was the two of them coming together that undid him.

He sidestepped one, only for the other to grab him in a bear hug. He managed to knee one in the groin. Then there followed a couple of heavy blows that took the wind out of him. Another one sent him crashing to the ground, where he took a bit of a kicking.

When he recovered enough to look up, it was to see one of the men dragging Sam and Kyle out of the house, both of them screaming. Sick at heart, he tried to get to his feet, only to receive another kicking.

Through his daze, he heard the main man confronting Sam and demanding in Russian to know the whereabouts of something or other. He wanted the key, as well. John understood that much, if not much else. But why ask her?

'Stop!' he croaked. 'It was me that took it. She can't tell you where it is. I'm the one—'

Another kick to the head scrambled his senses all over again and shut him up.

Sam screamed and hurled herself forward, trying to protect him. 'He doesn't know anything!' she insisted.

'It's down to you, then,' the main man said equably. 'Tell me where the key is. Tell me what I want to know. Then we will leave you in peace.'

'I don't think so,' Sam spat at him. 'You will kill us, just as you killed my father all those years ago.'

'You will tell us. Sooner or later, you will beg to tell us. I promise you that.'

Sam glowered at him.

John tried to follow what was going on, failingly miserably. Why wouldn't they listen to him? It was him, not Sam, they wanted.

Kuznetsov nodded to one of his men, who snatched Kyle away from Sam. She screamed and tried to reach her son but the other man pulled her by the hair and jammed a knee into her back to hold her off balance.

'You will tell us,' Kuznetsov said calmly. He took out a gun. 'First I shoot a few bullets into your man, and then I ask you again. If you still say no, then I kill him, and start on the boy. After that, we may have sex with you or not, but either way I will keep asking until you tell us what we want to know. Am I clear?'

Sam stared defiantly at him.

'OK. We start with him.'

Kuznetsov stepped forward and leant towards John, who stared into his eyes but found no comfort there. This man meant what he said.

The pistol in Kuznetsov's right hand spoke and John gasped and arched his back with the agony in his left arm.

'That's one arm,' Kuznetsov said with satisfaction. He straightened up, turned to a horrified, speechless Sam and said, 'Next a leg, do you think?'

Before she could speak, or scream, Kuznetsov's head exploded. Bone and other matter flew and spattered in all directions. Blood spouted out of his decapitated torso before it slumped to the ground.

John hurled himself sideways in a reflex action, long before his brain had begun to analyse what had just happened.

The pain from his shoulder convulsed him for a moment. When he looked up, he saw Sam standing frozen, horror stricken, and Kyle reaching for her.

Then he saw the two other men, both with guns in their hands. One started towards the door, only to collapse, arms flung wide, as if hit in the back by an avalanche. The second man collapsed a half second later, with half his head missing.

He gasped with shock. Blood and shit all over the place. In the background, he heard gunshots. The second man fell on top of him. By the time he had recovered enough to push him off, Sam had grabbed Kyle and was desperately trying to shield him with her body.

John struggled to his knees, then his feet and got himself upright. He glanced at the bodies all around him without understanding. Then he dived towards his wife and son, clamped his good arm around them and tried to push them towards the open doorway and into the house. Sam moved a short distance and then stood her ground. She wouldn't go any further.

He buried his face in her hair and briefly closed his eyes. When he opened them again, he saw that she was staring past him. He turned to see yet another man walking towards them, this one older and bulkier, and carrying a rifle.

CHAPTER TWENTY-NINE

It took Riley several hours, but eventually he thought he had found something. It wasn't much. Just an occasional boot mark pointing west. The same boot. One man. He guessed it was Tait.

By then, he was well out of the main search area. He pulled out his map and consulted it. Then he squinted into the distance. There was a little valley over there, and some sort of building near the head of it. Worth a look.

A little further on he came across more footprints, prints made by different boots. He nodded with satisfaction. It looked as though Tait had come this way. It also looked like Kuznetsov might be on to him. Interesting.

There was just the one building in the valley, an old stone farmhouse. It didn't look as if farm people lived there now. Working farms were surrounded by outbuildings, barns and equipment. Livestock even, and mud. This one wasn't. From his position high on the valley side, it looked empty and disused. Abandoned? Perhaps.

When he saw three figures manoeuvring down below, he brought out his scope and focused. One of them was Kuznetsov. He recognized him from the photo he'd sent Ted.

He nodded. His guess had been right. They had been on to him, and now they'd found him. Tait must be in the old farmhouse.

What now? He watched with interest as Kuznetsov approached the house, and the scene below began to unfold.

To his surprise, the woman and the boy appeared, as well as Tait. This was a long way for them to have come by themselves. How the hell had they managed it?

Well, here they were, along with Tait. And Kuznetsov and his buddies.

Some sort of discussion took place. Not negotiations. More a set of demands from Kuznetsov, it looked like. No doubt he wanted the money Tait had taken from Olsson. He was in a hurry. He'd come a long way for it. As near as he could make out, Tait told him to get lost.

Not very smart. Riley shook his head. Still, what else could he do? Tait was outnumbered. Worse than that, he was up against tough people, and handicapped by having his family with him. It was easy to see what was going to come next. Kuznetsov wasn't going to leave without the money, or some way of getting it.

Himself, in this situation, he would have threatened the wife or the kid, or both together. Not many family men would be able to withstand that sort of pressure. Instead, Kuznetsov was threatening the guy, Tait. It didn't make a lot of sense.

Tait's situation was pretty desperate. He would know none of them was going to be alive still when Kuznetsov left. There wasn't much doubt about that. So he would be playing for time, desperate to keep them all alive as long as he could.

The question, George Riley decided, was what, if anything, was he going to do about it? He sat back on his heels and mulled it over. Like Kuznetsov, seemingly, he wanted Tait dead — but only eventually. First, he wanted to know why he'd killed Jack Olsson. And he wanted to know what he'd done with the money as well.

Kuznetsov was fixing to shoot Tait, now they'd beaten him up a little. But if he let Kuznetsov shoot Tait, he would never get answers to those questions. They would stay with him, and bother him, forever more. Ted Pearson might be happy, but he wouldn't be.

Plus Kuznetsov looked like a nasty piece of shit anyway, just like his boss, Yugov. There wouldn't be anything good about what Kuznetsov and Yugov wanted.

With a reluctant sigh, he reached for his rifle.

CHAPTER THIRTY

'Inside,' the newcomer said, pointing with his rifle. 'It's kind of messy out here.'

Sam grabbed Kyle and rushed into the house.

John stood his ground. His vision was clearing and the pounding in his head was slowing. His shoulder was shrieking with pain but he tried to ignore it.

'You did this?' he asked, gesturing all around at the messiness.

'Inside,' the man said, pointing with his rifle. 'Now!'

John hesitated still. The tone wasn't friendly. If anything, it was icy. The newcomer might have saved his life, but he probably hadn't come with that in mind. It was just something that had happened. Inexplicable things happened on battlefields, and that's what this was — a battlefield.

'Who the hell are you?'

'Your guardian angel, maybe?'

'I don't think so. But thank you anyway. You saved my life.'

'For the moment. Now get inside.'

'They would have killed us all.'

'I know,' the newcomer said without much interest. 'But I couldn't let them do that. I wanted to talk to you first.'

It wasn't a very comforting explanation, but there was no doubt he owed the man. Also, the man had a rifle pointing at him. His shoulder wasn't good, either. He could feel blood running down his arm, as well as the pain. So he acceded and went inside to join his family.

'Ma'am,' the newcomer said, touching his hat with a forefinger, 'is there someplace else you can take your boy? I need to talk to your husband.'

'Of course,' Sam said calmly. 'We're in your debt. Thank you.'

John could see that she, too, was puzzled by the newcomer's icily polite manner. She understood well enough what he had done for them, though.

'Why do you want to talk to my husband alone?' she asked as she took Kyle by the hand.

'Ma'am,' he said patiently.

'Sam, just take Kyle upstairs out of the way,' John said gently. 'I'm OK with this.'

She looked questioningly at him. He nodded. She scooped up Kyle and headed for the stairs.

'So?' John said.

The rifle was still trained on him, he noted. This didn't look like it was going to be a very friendly conversation.

'That arm hurt much?'

'A bit.'

He was damned if he was going to admit it was throbbing like hell and worrying him a lot.

'Did you know those guys out there?' the man said, nodding over his shoulder.

'Not personally, no.'

'But you know who sent them?'

John nodded. There was no point lying. Better to get this over.

'My wife spotted their boss in the village. She recognized him. That's why she fled with our son. They're a bad bunch. Well, they were.'

'Amen to that. But you're no different, are you?'

'How's that?'

'I think you know what I'm getting at.'

John sighed wearily. 'So you, too, came for the money? How the hell did you all find out about it after all this time?'

The newcomer shook his head. 'What I want to know is why you killed Jack Olsson. So it was for the money, was it? Not for any other reason?'

The penny dropped. Ah! Jack Olsson, the name he had taken possession of for a few hours, many years ago. American, as was this man standing here in front of him. It was starting to make sense. Some of it, at least.

'I see the name is familiar to you?'

John nodded.

'Olsson was a colleague, and a friend of mine. Give me one good reason not to shoot you.'

The way the rifle settled ever more firmly in his arms, the way it was pointing ever more steadily at his chest, John knew the man was deadly serious. He was like the men he had just killed.

'I found Olsson's body,' he said steadily, 'but I wasn't the one who killed him.'

'No, of course you weren't.'

The man was unmoved. His gun never even wavered. The hands holding it were rock steady, the eyes behind them fixed and piercing.

John tried again. 'I simply found myself in the wrong place at the wrong time.'

'Yep. You got that part right. And now you've done it again.'

'Look, I admit I took the money. But by then it was no good to him. He was already dead when I found him.'

'Yeah.'

He sensed the man was running out of patience. He could see his finger tightening its hold on the trigger. This wasn't someone you could bluff or argue with. The evidence for that was just outside the door. What else could he tell him, he thought desperately.

All he could think of doing was to try to tell it like it had been, back there in a time he had almost, but not quite, managed to forget.

'You don't know how it was for me at that time,' he said, taking a deep breath. 'I'd been running for twenty-four hours. People after me — like the ones you just shot. No money. Nothing, in fact, but the clothes on my back, and a car I'd stolen off the street in Lviv. I was desperate.

'I stopped at this crummy little ski chalet because it looked cheap. I had ten euros in my pocket, just enough to pay for a night there. There was only one other guest, and he turned out to be dead.

'Just after five in the morning I was on my way out, ready to start running again. I saw him still sitting in a chair, like he had been the night before. I went into his room to see if he was all right, and I saw he had a bullet hole in his head. There was nothing I could do for him.

'When I looked for a passport, or an ID card, to see who he was, I started finding money and passports galore. I realized I'd found a lifeline.' He paused, shrugged and added, 'What would you have done, in my circumstances? Called the cops?'

After a long pause, the man said, 'Where were you running from? And why?'

'Lviv, in Ukraine. I worked for a businessman there. A Russian gang came through — sent by the same guy as that lot out there, in fact! — and murdered him and everyone they could find. They wanted control of his businesses in the east, amongst other things. I was just lucky enough not to be there when they called.'

'The guy you worked for? What was his name?'

'Sirko, Viktor Sirko.'

He could see it was a name that meant something. The man knew, or had known, of Sirko. He felt a glimmer of hope for a moment. Then it died.

'I don't believe you. You're full of shit.'

'It's the truth,' he said doggedly.

'Give me one good reason not to pull the trigger right now.'

John shrugged helplessly. He had already played his only card.

'Maybe I can!' a voice called from the stairs.

'Keep out of it, lady! Look after your boy.'

'I can prove my husband is telling the truth.'

'Get back upstairs. You're wasting my time here.'

'You need to listen to me.'

'And why is that?'

'I am Vlasta Sirko,' she said defiantly, 'the daughter of Viktor Sirko, if that means anything to you.'

'Well, well! Fancy that,' the man murmured.

John stared at Sam, aghast at her intervention. She was putting herself in the line of fire.

'Sam!' he began to protest. 'The man's right. Look after Kyle.'

She overrode him, ignored him.

'I know my husband is telling the truth, because I, too, was in Lviv when the Russians came. I know exactly what they did there.'

The man's eyes strayed at last, to stare at Sam for a moment.

'OK,' he said. 'I guess you'd better tell me the rest of the story. But first, let's take a look at your husband's arm.'

CHAPTER THIRTY-ONE

'I'm John Tait, but I suppose you know my name.'

'Yeah. George Riley.'

With Riley's help, John peeled off his jacket and blood-soaked shirt. Sam found a First Aid kit, army issue. Working together, she and Riley staunched the bleeding and cleaned the wound, and then bandaged it.

'You were lucky,' Riley said. 'It will hurt a bit for a while, but no bone damage. Just soft tissue.'

'It was intended to be just the start of things,' John said grimly.

'Yeah. He planned on shooting you a bit at a time. Wouldn't have taken him long, either.'

He tore the blood-soaked sleeve off John's shirt and discarded it. 'What I would like to know,' he said in a conversational aside to Sam, 'is what those guys wanted from you.'

Sam shrugged.

John wondered if she was hiding something. He looked at her. 'Sam, what is it?'

'Let's just sort ourselves out,' she said briskly. 'Everything else can wait. I'm going to see to Kyle now.'

'So what did you do with the money?' Riley asked, sitting down at the kitchen table. 'I haven't seen any sign of it.'

Joining him, John sighed and said, 'I've still got most of it. I couldn't find a safe and legal way of spending it.'

'That's honest. So, you worked for old Viktor, eh?'

'I did. He was a good man. If he hadn't got himself killed, he could well have been president by now.'

'Maybe.' Riley frowned and added, 'Jack Olsson was on his way to see Sirko, or on his way back. If you didn't kill him, who did?'

'No idea. I've wondered that for a long time. What puzzled me at first was that whoever did it hadn't taken the money. Then it occurred to me that someone else must be coming along for the money, and I'd better get out before they arrived.'

'Yugov?'

'I didn't know that then, but I do now.'

Riley nodded.

They both looked round then, as Sam came down the stairs. 'Kyle is sleeping,' she said. 'Would you like me to make some coffee?'

'Sure,' Riley said. 'Then you can tell me what those fellas out there wanted so badly from you.'

Sam made coffee for them all, and then she sat down alongside her husband, across the table from the man who had saved their lives.

'So,' Riley said. 'Where is the key? And what's it for?'

John had been wondering about that himself. It bothered him that Sam seemed to have kept something secret from him. But that was how it was, and Yugov knew of it.

Another thing, he thought. Kuznetsov had made no mention of the money, and he had discounted him. He'd been ready to write him off, in fact. It had been Sam he wanted. What the hell was this key he'd been demanding?

'Not the key to the lock up?' he asked her now. 'Where the money is?'

She gave a small shake of her head and looked down.

Riley gave her a moment to consider. Then he said, 'You'd better tell us.'

She didn't reply.

'Suit yourself, lady, but silence ain't going to do you or your family any good. Yugov will still be around, and he can soon replace the men he lost here. They want that key pretty bad, it seems to me. They won't give up.'

'What about you?' Sam said defiantly. 'What do you want?'

'Me?' He stared at her for a moment. 'I'm here to shoot your husband. That's my job.'

'Why? He knows nothing!'

'For killing Jack Olsson. My boss wants him dead. Tell me about this key and maybe I won't shoot him. It's your choice.'

It was unnerving, John thought, how he could sit there drinking their coffee and talking like that. But he'd never let go of his rifle. It wouldn't do to underestimate him, or start thinking they were in the clear.

'You're comfortable with it — your job, I mean?' he asked mildly.

'I've been doing it a long time, son. Killing people don't mean so much to me.'

'I feel sorry for you!' Sam said bitterly.

Riley shrugged. He wasn't here to make friends, the gesture seemed to imply.

'There is no bloody key!' John said suddenly, fiercely, resenting how the discussion was developing. 'I can tell you that now. If there is, she doesn't have it! We don't know what the hell they were talking about.'

'Maybe you don't, but she does,' Riley said, rapping the table with his rifle. 'She knows. If she values your life, as I suspect she does, she'll tell me. Otherwise . . .' He finished with another shrug.

'What?' John said, stung. 'You think you can take me?'

'Probably.'

'I may only have one good arm at the moment, but . . .'

He grabbed for the rifle. Riley batted his hand away with it.

'Stop it!' Sam snapped. 'Stop it now, both of you.'

'That's better!' Riley chuckled, amused.

She shook her head and said wearily, 'Yes, I do know about the key.'

'Rubbish!' John said heatedly. 'Stay out of it, for God's sake.'

'No, John. I can't, not now. I've tried, but I can't do it any longer.'

'Sam, you don't know what you're saying!'

'I do. I wish I didn't, but I do.'

'What's the key to?' Riley asked quickly.

She took a deep breath and said, 'The entrance to a cave.'

'Where is this cave?'

'Sam!' John snapped, horrified.

She shook her head at him, and said, 'It's in Ukraine.'

Riley nodded with satisfaction, thinking now they were getting somewhere. Sweet Jesus. This promised to be something special.

'What's in the cave?' he asked.

She shook her head. It was a question too far, for the moment at least. She had admitted enough.

He didn't bother asking where the key was. That would come out eventually. A cave, eh? What the hell was in it? Something important, something valuable. All Sirko's earthly possessions, perhaps?

'What's in it?' he asked again.

'Weapons,' John said bleakly. 'Armaments.'

Sam threw him an agonized glance. He ignored it.

'I always knew there was such a place, somewhere,' he added. 'I just didn't know where it was, or that my wife knew about it.'

'That true?' Riley asked Sam.

She nodded.

'Right, lady,' Riley said decisively, laying the rifle aside at last. 'Pick up your boy. Let's go home. We have a lot to talk about, and this isn't my idea of the best place to do it.'

CHAPTER THIRTY-TWO

Before they left, the two men took a couple of spades from the tool collection in an outhouse and buried the bodies a little distance away from the house. It was hard work, and illegal, but it had to be done. They couldn't afford either to report the deaths or allow them to be discovered. Too much was at stake.

The ground was hard, despite the surface mud and water, and the soil thin. A pick would have made for faster progress than spades alone, but they didn't have one.

'I'm getting too old for this kind of thing,' Riley complained, pausing for a rest.

'Done a lot of it, have you?'

'More than my share.'

John could believe that. The other man was no innocent abroad.

'Maybe you have, too?' Riley added.

John shrugged and said, 'I thought I was finished with all this ten years ago.'

'Yeah. You and me both. I was living happily in retirement until I got the call.'

'About Olsson?'

'Yeah. Like I said, he was a friend as well as a colleague.'

They shut up then, and got the job done. After that, they collected Sam and Kyle, and started the journey home.

'You'll forgive me,' Riley said, when they reached the house, 'if I ask that one of you is always here with me in the kitchen.'

They both looked at him.

He said, 'I don't want to risk you two conspiring against me. I don't want even the possibility of that.'

John snorted with derision.

Sam said, 'We understand. It is better this way, I think. We must all show our cards on the table, yes?'

Riley nodded. 'That's it. Much better if we understand each other, and can trust what's being said.'

John shrugged. If that was what they both wanted, it didn't bother him. It made a kind of sense, he supposed.

'Is your boy ready for bed?' Riley asked Sam.

'He is.'

'Then put him to bed. We'll talk when you're done.'

The two men sat around the kitchen table, just as they had in the old farmhouse. They sat largely in silence, waiting for Sam to return.

'You hungry?' John asked.

'Not especially. You?'

John shook his head. 'Let's get the conversation going. We can eat later.'

Sam returned, took a seat at the table and looked at the two men expectantly.

'I'm George,' Riley said in a friendly manner. 'He's John. How do you like to be called, ma'am?'

'I used to be Vlasta, but I've been Sam for a long time now. So call me Sam.'

'Fair enough. So now we've got the introductions out of the way.'

'Not quite,' John said. 'You know who we are, but who are you? Who do you represent?'

'I'll be frank with you, John. I'm a retired United States intelligence agent — it doesn't matter exactly who I work

139

for. Right now, I represent Jack Olsson. Nobody else. I came here, at the request of our old boss, to seek justice for Jack.'

'Justice?'

'I came to take you out, John. Let me be frank about that, too. Washington had information, at last, that seemed to tell us what had happened to old Jack all those years ago. I came to put it all to rights.'

'That's honest,' John said, shaking his head.

'Yeah. But first I wanted to check that the info was correct. It wasn't. Somebody else — not you, I now believe — killed Jack. So,' he added, raising his hands, palms out to them, 'here we are.'

There was a few moments pause while these initial exchanges were absorbed. Then George said, 'What about this cave, Sam? What can you tell us about it? I believe it may have something to do with why Jack was killed.'

Both men gazed at her. She gathered her thoughts and touched the back of John's hand with her fingers, as if in apology.

'My father had considerable business interests, as you probably know. After the dissolution of the Soviet Union, after Ukraine became independent, he built up his business empire very successfully. He had many interests. Inevitably,' she added with a shrug, 'some were concerned with the arms trade. That was not illegal. It was just another business. My husband was recruited and employed by my father for a time as a security consultant. John could provide a western perspective, and my father felt he needed that.'

'Perspective on what?' George asked sceptically. 'The arms trade?'

John shook his head. 'That came into it a little, but mostly it was defence and economic strategy. I'd been involved in that sort of work for the British Government, after military service, but defence cuts after the end of the Cold War meant that a lot of people like me in military intelligence were made redundant. I had to do something for a living, and Viktor made me a very good offer. I enjoyed working for him, too, until it all went pear-shaped.'

'And you really didn't know about this cave?'

John shook his head. 'I had an idea that something like it existed. Just from bits of information I picked up here and there. But that was all. I didn't know where it was, or what was in it in any detail.'

Sam winced, as if she felt now that she should have been more forthcoming with him. John tried to disregard it.

'The cave?' George said, looking at her.

'It is a very dangerous place.'

'Because?'

'Because it is a place where my father stored a lot of military equipment and weapons, a very secret place.'

'Not secret enough, though, if Yugov knows of it.'

She nodded. 'That is true, but he can't know much. His big mistake was that when he attacked my father's headquarters he killed everyone who knew the cave's location. Except me,' she added.

'And you have the key to the door, as well as knowing the location, which is why he has come all this way?'

Sam nodded.

'You've said nothing all these years,' John said in a rebuke he couldn't help making.

'I'm sorry, John. I just didn't like to think about it, and I believed it would be better if the cave's existence was forgotten. No good could come of anyone finding it, and accessing all those weapons.

'In time, I did forget about it. At least, I stopped thinking about it. There was so much happening. We had a new life here, and then Kyle arrived. There was no need to mention a cave full of guns in a region we were never likely to visit.'

'Be that as it may,' George said, 'somehow the knowledge has been resurrected, and has come to Yugov's attention. And, by coincidence, Yugov has discovered where you people live, just as that was discovered in Washington. Isn't that curious?'

'Must have been a leak,' John said heavily. 'It's no coincidence.'

George nodded. 'I agree.'

He went on to tell them of Olsson's body being identified, and of the DNA evidence linking John to it.

'All this might never have happened,' George concluded, 'if your burglar, a few months ago, had chosen another house to raid.'

They discussed the process of discovery for a while. Then George said, 'Where is this damned cave that Yugov wants so very badly?'

'In Ukraine,' Sam said, 'western Ukraine.'

'Not the east, where all the fighting has been going on?'

She shook her head. 'If it was there, Yugov wouldn't have had a problem reaching it. The Russians control that area now.'

'Well,' George said thoughtfully, 'anyone got a map handy?'

CHAPTER THIRTY-THREE

John brought out *The Times Atlas of the World* initially. He opened it to a page showing Ukraine, as well as a big chunk of Russia and a few other countries as well.

'Here,' Sam said, pointing to a spot just north of Moldova, one of the countries bordering Ukraine.

'Close to the Carpathian mountains,' George said, poring over the map.

'Not that close,' John said with a frown. 'It's probably thirty miles away.'

'It is in the Dniester valley,' Sam confirmed.

'Not my backyard,' George said thoughtfully. 'The Dniester? That's the river that runs down through Ukraine and Moldova to the Black Sea, right?'

'Yes,' Sam said. 'On the way, it separates Transnistria from most of Moldova.'

'This little itty, bitty strip of land east of the river that wants to be forever part of the Soviet Union?' George mused. 'I heard about that territory.'

'They are Russian speakers there,' Sam said. 'Like in eastern Ukraine.'

'Yeah.'

George was thinking. Transnistria was somewhere else Jack Olsson had been asked to poke his nose into, in the hope they could get the Russian nationalists there to rally to the dollar. Fat chance! Forget it. Those guys were still Stalin's children.

'I heard something about an arms dump in that area,' John contributed, still focused on the Dniester valley. 'But not from you, Sam!'

'What good would it have done if I had told you?' Sam protested. 'My father told me I was the only other person with the key. I wanted to keep it that way. From what he told me, I wanted the cave to be forgotten — forever!'

'Children, children!' George said mildly. 'Let's not squabble, please.'

John clamped his lips firmly together for a moment. Sam and George were both right, but that didn't stop him feeling pissed off about the whole damned thing. No secrets, they had promised each other!

Still, he reminded himself, they were in a hole. Best to stop digging. Sam had only done what she thought was right. He should be supporting her. Maybe this was a secret she had been safeguarding him from.

'Down there,' he said, making an effort, 'it's karst country. Limestone. I know about that sort of landscape from my time in what used to be Yugoslavia.'

'Yeah? You and me both,' George said with a wry chuckle. 'You have been around, young man.'

'I never went to the Dniester valley, though,' John added. 'Viktor can't have trusted me enough. But I've heard it's a pretty special area.' He gave a thoughtful frown. 'Caves. Lots of caves.'

'Including the Gypsum Giants,' Sam said.

'What the hell are they?' George wanted to know.

'Caves that have been hollowed out of the gypsum rock over many millions of years. I don't know,' Sam said with a shrug, 'but some people say they are the biggest caves in the world. The biggest gypsum caves, at least. In the war against the fascists—'

'The what?' George interrupted.

'World War Two,' John said quickly. 'That's what some people out there still call it.'

'Thank you, John!' Sam said with a wry smile. 'In World War Two, there were Jewish refugees who lived in the caves there, and escaped the holocaust.'

'What?' George said. 'Lived there for four years?'

'Yes!' she responded quickly. 'There have been people living in some of those caves for half a million years. At least, so the archaeologists say.'

'Rather them than me,' George said, shaking his head. 'Cold and damp, caves. And dark. So that's where your daddy hid his Kalashnikovs?'

'More than that, I think.'

'Oh?'

Sam shrugged. 'Almost anything you can think of that has a military use. And some things, I believe, it is better not to know about.'

'Like what?' George said fast.

'Like I said, it is better you don't know. Better for you, better for us and better for the rest of the world.'

George looked up at John, who shrugged and said, 'Don't ask me! I don't know. But if Sam believes that, we should listen to her.'

George didn't press them. 'You got a larger scale map of the area?' he asked instead.

'Somewhere,' John said. 'I'll see if I can find it.'

From the large-scale map they could see that the land north of the Dniester was pretty level and low-lying, while the southern bank of the river was where the hill country started.

'These cliffs,' Sam said, pointing to the south side of the river, 'are made of limestone. They are full of holes and passages — and caves, of course.'

'I know a bit about karst country,' George said. 'We have some in the States, down in Tennessee and a few other places. And like John, here, I was in Yugoslavia for a while, where the Serbs hid their whole damn army in caves.

'What happens is the rainwater penetrates the surface of the rock, erodes away at it through cracks and faults, and forms caverns. Some of those things can go a long way underground.'

'Exactly,' Sam said. 'The Gypsum Giants have been explored for hundreds of kilometres, but even now no one knows how far they go.'

'Far and deep,' George said, nodding. 'Easy to get lost in them suckers, and easy to hide stuff away. Were you ever in your daddy's cave?'

'Once. He wanted to show me where it was. Once was enough.'

She broke off and shuddered at the memory.

'Viktor wasn't the only one who was storing weapons underground,' John said suddenly, remembering. 'When the trouble got going in eastern Ukraine the other year, it turned out the Red Army had left behind an arms dump in an old salt mine near Slavyansk. There were 3,000,000 firearms in that one. Local people blockaded it for a while, to try to stop anyone using the weapons.'

'I remember reading about that,' George said. 'But the separatists probably got it all in the end. The question for us, though, is who was Viktor Sirko storing arms for — the government in Kiev, or the Rebs? He sure didn't need them for himself.'

They sat in silence for a few moments, pondering the implications of that question.

'And what does Yugov want with them?' John mused.

'Oh, that's easy,' George said. 'He'll just sell them to the highest bidder, if he can get his hands on them.'

He turned to Sam and said, 'How safe is that key? Where do you keep it?'

She shrugged. 'In my head.'

'So it's not a physical key?'

She shook her head. 'It's a set of numbers for a keypad. It took me many months to learn them, and I have never forgotten them.'

George sighed heavily and said, 'So you really are important to Yugov. You are the key, literally.'

There was another, more protracted silence. Then John said, 'So when are we going?'

CHAPTER THIRTY-FOUR

'John!' Sam cried, scandalized. 'You can't possibly go there. And I can't, either.'

'Think about it,' he said evenly. 'How will we ever get Yugov off our backs? As long as that secret arms dump exists, you'll be in danger. He knows you have the key. He knows you know where the cave is. He knows where we live! Work it out.'

Sam pushed her chair back, sprang to her feet and rushed out of the room.

John and George sat in silence, not looking at each other.

'Go to her,' George said eventually. 'Go to your wife and son. They need you.'

'We have an agreement. One of us stays with you at all times. Remember?'

George shook his head. 'It doesn't matter now. Besides, I need to make a phone call to Washington.'

John stared at him.

'I may tell you about it later,' George said with a wry smile. 'But you no longer have anything to worry about from me. I can tell you that much.'

John nodded and got up to go and find Sam.

George knew he was taking a gamble, but he'd decided. He was going for it. He'd watched the Taits for a while, unbeknown to them, and he had seen how they lived. They lived well, modestly and hardworking, but well. He liked that. He liked them. It wouldn't be him that made Sam a widow, and young Kyle a fatherless little boy.

Also, he was inclined to believe John Tait about the sad business back in Slovakia all those years ago. The man could well have been a killer back then. Probably was, in fact. But he wasn't now. More important, he didn't believe Tait had killed Jack Olsson.

The story John had told had been simple, unrehearsed and wholly credible. It was not hard to imagine how stressed he had been in his desperate flight from Lviv. His friends and colleagues, his boss even, had all been murdered by Yugov's marauders. He himself had escaped by the skin of his teeth, warned by the woman who was now his wife.

He had somehow managed to get out, but had been able to carry nothing with him. Falling back on his wits and mental strength, he had escaped. Then had come the extraordinary discovery of Jack Olsson, and all that cash.

George shook his head. Pure coincidence? Well, it was hard to come to any other conclusion. Tait's one concern had been to evade whatever pursuit was after him. Virtually penniless, and exhausted, he had done the best he could and crossed the border. Even then, though, he wouldn't have felt safe. Russians, especially the likes of Yugov, never had been great respecters of borders.

Even if he had encountered Jack Olsson while Jack was still alive, he would have had no reason to shoot him, and even less to imagine he was carrying $10,000,000. Much more likely was that someone else had known who Jack was, and what he was carrying.

So he was satisfied with the Taits. Now he had something to do with them, something in which they had a shared interest. First, though, he needed to talk to Ted, back in DC. Tait was right. Somebody back there probably had leaked the information that had brought both himself and Yugov to this little town. Ted needed to know that. Ted needed to find the culprit.

Right now, though, there was something else that needed looking into. Ted could wait a little while.

When George stepped outside, the weather had changed, changed for the better. The rain and the wind had died away, the dank humid conditions had dispersed. In the late afternoon the sky was clear and he felt that soon there would be frost. That suited him fine. Cold, clean air was what he liked best. Visibility was better then, too.

He headed down the garden, checking the ground as he went. There were all sorts of footprints after the previous night's heavy rain but he wasn't looking for them. Something else was on his mind. He was thinking blood. But he didn't find any.

At the foot of the garden he stood by the gate for a few moments, looking around. There was woodland beyond the stone wall that marked the boundary of the Tait property, but the leading edge was a good fifty yards away, and uphill. Too far, and too hard to get there.

Where would a badly injured man head for, assuming he was capable of moving at all?

The Tait property was separated from its neighbour on one side by a rampant, wild hedge of hawthorn, bramble and occasional small trees that had developed from the seeds left by bird droppings. George walked the length of it, peering into the shadows at the base of the hedge. Nothing. He saw nothing out of the ordinary at all.

It was always possible that the man had recovered and departed, or that someone had come and collected him, but he didn't think so somehow. He had seen one of the man's colleagues drop back to check on him, and then give it up and join the chase after Tait. The man had been too badly injured. That was George's conclusion at the time. He still thought it was right.

The other side of the Tait property was marked by a continuation of the stone wall that ran along the foot of the garden. George walked the length of that, too, again without finding anything. Perhaps he was wrong? He still didn't think so.

He hoisted himself up on to the wall and peered at the rough grass dotted with gorse on the other side. Plenty of cover, if you could get that far. Out of the question, though, for a badly injured man. In that condition, the wall would be an insurmountable obstacle.

Then he heard a groan that proved him wrong. Glancing sideways, he saw a figure sprawled in the shadow of the wall, not ten yards away. Quickly, he climbed over the wall and approached the figure cautiously, pistol in hand. The man was seated with his back leaning against the wall. George could see his eyes watching his approach.

George stopped and peered down at him. He was in a bad way. That much was obvious. In need of intensive care, but probably beyond it anyway. There was no spilled blood visible. George guessed he had at least a fractured skull. How the hell had he got over the wall? Russians, he thought with a sigh.

'Speak English?' he asked quietly.

'*Nyet*. Hospital!'

So he did. He spoke at least some of the language.

'You hurting?'

'Bad, bad. Hurt bad.'

George nodded sympathetically. 'Your colleagues left you here, huh?'

There was no response. The man closed his eyes.

'They are dead. You know that? Those guys that were with you? I shot them.'

The eyes opened again. Stared right back. George nodded, confirming it.

'What about the others?' he asked. 'Will they come for you? Yugov, perhaps?'

It didn't seem like he was going to get an answer. Then the man's lips muttered something.

'Say again?' George said, leaning closer.

'Hospital — please!'

'In a minute. Where's Yugov? Is he coming back for you? Won't he take you?'

'Yugov gone. No come back.'

'Gone? Where?'

'Back to Ukraine. Hospital — now!'

'In a minute, old son. You just hang on there.'

Gone? Could that be true? If it was, what did it mean?

It seemed to mean Yugov had decided he didn't need to wait any longer. He must have believed his men would catch up with Tait and Sirko's daughter. Was that it? Or had he decided he didn't need them anymore? Had he got what he wanted some other way?

'What about the cave?' George asked gently. 'Doesn't he need to know where it is?'

'He knows. Now he knows.'

'How? Who told him?'

'Hospital,' the man implored again.

George thought fast. This changed things. He was sure it was true, as well. Yugov would surely have stayed otherwise.

'So Yugov knows everything? He knows where the cave is, and he has the key?'

'No key, not yet. Just where the cave is. Hospital!'

George patted him on the shoulder. 'I'm going to help you now,' he said. 'Don't you worry, comrade.'

The eyes closed gratefully.

As he straightened up, George brought the pistol swiftly round from his side and shot the man in the back of the head. One shot. It sounded loud, so loud that a flock of rooks sprawled out of their roost in the neighbouring trees, filling the air with the sound of their alarm.

CHAPTER THIRTY-FIVE

George let himself back into the kitchen, where John was sitting at the table with another mug of coffee.

'Help yourself,' John said, nodding towards the kettle.

'Thanks. I will. Sam OK?'

'Yeah. She's worried, that's all.'

John nodded, and waited until George had made himself some coffee and sat down with it before saying, 'Was that noise what I thought it was?'

'Nothing to be done for him, and we have to get a move on.' George shrugged and stirred his coffee. 'Yugov has left. And he knows where the cave is.'

'How did that happen? More information leaked?'

'It sounds like it,' George said wearily. 'But I don't know. All I know is we've got to get there fast, if we're going to stop him.'

'That's a big ask, George. Why us?'

'Because we know what's going on. Can you imagine how long it would take to persuade the "proper authorities" to do something — even if they could?'

'But you think we can do something?'

'We can try.'

'Yeah. We can try,' John said wearily. 'But if Yugov knows where the cave is, it's a different proposition now.'

'We'll get help,' George said brusquely. 'From somewhere, we'll get help. But we need to get there fast if we're going to stop him.'

John nodded. 'What did you say that noise was again?'

'I didn't. But between you and me, it would be better if Sam and Kyle don't look over that garden wall, out there, for a while. I've phoned for body removal this time,' he added.'

'The guy I hit?'

George nodded.

'I see. I'm surprised he was still there.'

'He was too badly injured for Yugov to attempt to recover him, and it would have been too dangerous to tell anyone about him. So they left him to get on with it.'

'They just dumped him over the wall?'

'Who knows?'

John reflected a moment, and then said, 'He told you all this?'

'Some of it. He told me what he knew. And now we know we gotta get moving.'

'So we're going to Ukraine. When — tomorrow?'

'Tomorrow, John. You'd better tell Sam.'

John winced. 'She's not going to like it.'

'Even so. We need the location of the cave and the key, and she can't go herself. You know that.'

It was true. Her passport was no longer valid. His own would expire soon, too. Then there was Kyle to consider. One of them had to stay for that reason alone.

'Sam here legally?' George asked.

'Not yet.'

'You'd better see to that as well, son. You don't want to risk losing her.'

John nodded. 'I will, just as soon as this thing is over. It's long overdue. We've been living in our own little bubble these past ten years, scared to move in case we might do something to burst it.'

'You know what to do. I'm not gonna say another word.'

'Thanks, George!' John said, laughing.

CHAPTER THIRTY-SIX

The entrance to the main cave couldn't have been a secret, even though it was shielded by a thin belt of woodland. If anything, it was like the entrance to a railway tunnel — very obvious. There was even a rough track winding its way up to it from the forestry road below. Its very ordinariness might have been some protection, John thought, as he and George made their way through the portals. There were many such caves in the area, some of them with much larger entrances than this one. They had seen a few.

They made their way some fifty yards into the cave, passing through a huge vault-like space before continuing along a narrower passage that was still wide and high enough to accommodate a big truck. There were no tracks on the cave floor, but that meant nothing after ten years of disuse. Even back then when the cave was being used, sweeping the floor upon exit would probably have been mandatory in a secret facility.

'Reminds me of Serbia,' George said conversationally. 'This kind of country, you can conceal an entire army without any difficulty whatsoever.'

'And the Serbs did,' John pointed out.

'That's right. They did. The US Air Force couldn't find 'em to bomb. Buildings all over the country were toppled and blown up, but we never laid a finger on any of their military capability. When it was all over, they came out of the caves and tunnels, with their tanks and armoured personnel carriers, laughing at us.'

'Yeah. They didn't have many communication towers left, though, did they?'

'Not one,' George said with apparent satisfaction.

'Just a pity about the tanks, and things.'

'Don't try my patience anymore, young fella,' George growled.

They moved on and turned left, into a side passage that led after another hundred yards to a massive steel door. There was no obvious way of opening the door. It simply stood there, big and solid, a sheet of unadorned steel, nothing on it whatsoever.

John thumped the door with the heel of his hand. There was no vibration, no sound or echo, or any other indication that the door had registered their presence.

'Impressive.'

He looked at George, who nodded and said quietly, 'This is it. We got here. Now let's see if we can get the sucker open.'

'I can't see us getting any reception in here, all this way underground.'

'Maybe it doesn't work like a normal cell phone?' George suggested.

John shrugged. 'We'll soon find out.'

He punched the long list of digits Sam had given him into his phone. Then he checked to make sure he had got the list correct. Finally, he pressed "Send".

Nothing happened.

For agonizing seconds, half a minute or so, nothing seemed to happen. Then they heard a series of clicks and a whirring sound from somewhere, and slowly the great steel sheet began to slide aside. It revealed a wall of blackness that the battery lamps they were carrying barely penetrated. As they stared into the void, strip lights began to flicker, one after another in two parallel lines. Within a few more moments the world beyond the door was brightly lit.

They both stared in silence, astonished, for a long moment. Then John said breathlessly, 'Oh my God! Just look at it.'

George said nothing. He just stared.

It wasn't an arms dump the like John had ever seen, or even imagined. There was a whole new world beyond the door, a city at least, a grid-iron city. Not a populated city, but still one with roads and lane markings. They could see an array of fork-lift trucks, scores of them, in a parking area close to the entrance, ready to start servicing long lines of storage racks stacked perhaps thirty feet high.

They both stood and stared, astounded and temporarily speechless. Somewhere a generator started up, ignited by invisible hands. The lights began to shine even more brightly.

Eventually, John shook his head and said, 'Viktor Sirko's private doomsday enabler.'

'Something like that,' George agreed. 'Come on! Let's take a look around.'

John eyed the edge of the door, now recessed into the wall of the cave, and said uneasily, 'If that thing closes with us inside, we'll never get back out.'

'It ain't gonna do that, my friend.' George chuckled. 'What we're looking at here is a marvel of American civil engineering, US Army engineering. Built to last, and without a malfunction option. This place will still be in perfect order when there's no one left alive on the planet.'

John snorted scornfully, but he suspected George might be right. Who else could have done all this? Who else but the US Army could have installed moving parts that were still working after more than ten years in hibernation, without the aid of an external power source? NASA? Maybe it was a practice for colonizing Mars.

'What are we looking for specifically?' John asked.

George shook his head. 'We'll know it when we see it, I guess. Whatever it is, it sure scared your wife.'

That was true, John thought. He had never known Sam so tight lipped and worried.

She just wouldn't talk about it. He had given up trying to get more out of her. It had to be something really nasty.

Swallowing their inhibitions, they moved forward together and entered Viktor Sirko's lost world of defence equipment and assault weapons.

They walked together, side by side, up and down the aisles of what was an enormous military warehouse. The sheer scale of it reduced them to awed silence. They walked past rows of shelves containing small arms, heavy machine guns, field artillery, mortars, and crates of ammunition. Then there were battle tanks and armoured troop carriers, and jeeps and trucks. And mountains of miscellaneous equipment, and boots and clothing. Enough for at least an army. Nothing bore insignias but there might as well have been a white star on everything.

'Enough to fit an army,' John remarked, bewildered, as they walked back towards the entrance.

'A helluva big army,' George agreed. 'Maybe more than one.'

'Viktor might have owned or managed this dump, but I don't believe he set it up. This place is way too big for his organization.'

George nodded. 'You're right.'

'I wonder what he intended doing with all this stuff anyway.'

'Who?' George asked cynically. 'Sirko, the Chief of the General Staff or the President of the United States of America?'

John shrugged. It was a fair question. And he had no idea. Couldn't even begin to guess.

He came to a halt. 'Mind if we split up for a few minutes, George? I want to check one or two things.'

'You're not thinking of offloading a couple of tanks, are you?'

John grinned. 'I'll see you back at the entrance in twenty minutes.'

So far as he could tell, the cave was a couple of hundred feet below ground. At first glance, that gave it cover against any sort of strike except a deep bunker-penetrating nuclear missile. It was a hell of a facility.

He made his way over to one of the walls and started to follow it, using his lamp to check the condition of the wall. It was mostly sound. There were places where the limestone had crumbled, but those places had been patched up with concrete.

The cave roof looked pretty sound, too. He couldn't see any signs of imminent collapse anywhere. In fact, the cave looked clean and new. Judging by the markings left in the rock by machinery, it wasn't wholly natural.

There might have been a small cave to begin with, but most of this place had been carved out of the solid rock by engineers. He could see the patterns in the roof and walls, the squirls and whorls, made by the big drilling machine they had used. The mole would have bored its way in from the entrance cave, and now would be resting in perpetuity somewhere in the furthest reaches of the cave. Those things got built *in situ*, and never came out of the tunnels they dug.

It had been a big project, and somehow it had been undertaken in secrecy. How the hell had Viktor had managed to keep it so quiet?

He shook his head. He had no idea, and he'd seen enough for now. He made his way back to the entrance, where George was leaning against a wall, waiting patiently.

'You done here?'

John nodded. 'For now. Let's close it up again. I'd like to take a quick look up on top. Then I suggest we go somewhere and discuss what we've seen.'

George nodded. 'Suits me. Let's get the hell out of here.'

Back outside, George left John to climb up the steep slope to the top of the cliff, while he ambled back to the Range Rover they had hired in Kiev.

'Half an hour max,' John said. 'OK?'

'Take your time. I can wait to hear what you've got in mind.'

John nodded. He did have something in mind, but everything depended on what he found topside.

He made his way up the snow-covered hillside, scrambling over rock outcrops and expanses of scree and gravel, threading his way through the thin coniferous woodland. It was cold, a few degrees below zero, but the temperature was welcome. Cold, clean, fresh air was something he had craved back there in the cave.

On top, under a thin snow cover, the surface was old, weathered limestone, with a sparse scatter of pine trees and dead grass on gravelly soil. As he moved around he found craters and holes aplenty. Typical karst landscape. Some of the holes were deep. He dropped pebbles into a few of the more promising of them, and counted the seconds until he heard the pebbles hit the bottom.

When he came away, he was well satisfied. What he had been thinking might well be possible. If they got to that point, he might be able to make a reality of Sam's most fervent wish.

CHAPTER THIRTY-SEVEN

'Well,' George said, 'what did you get out of that?'

John shook his head ruefully. 'What a place! Viktor certainly kept it well quiet. Sam, too.'

'Don't be too hard on her. She did what she thought was best. If she was the only living person who knew where it was, and nobody but you knew where she was . . .'

'Yeah. I know. It should have been a secret forever. Except it doesn't work like that, does it?'

'Not very often, no. The truth will out, as they say.'

'There was a lot of interesting stuff in there,' John said, reflectively. 'A lot of dangerous stuff, too.'

'Yep. Toxic, poisonous, flammable, explosive — some of it real nasty — and plain ordinary bullets, bombs and missiles.'

John poured them both more coffee from a big flask. 'Most of it with US Army markings,' he said. 'Do you know any of the codes they use, or will we have to open boxes and crates to find out what's in them?'

'Some. I recognized some of 'em.' George gave a wry chuckle. 'And I sure as hell know a main battle tank when I see one!'

'You and me both,' John said ruefully. 'Jesus! They could fight a really big war with what's in there.'

George nodded solemnly. 'You figured out a way of closing it down yet, getting rid of it all?'

'Possibly. Is that what you would like to happen?'

'It is, considering what I saw in there. There was some very unpleasant stuff in that cave, stuff I wouldn't want to see used on anyone.'

'Chemicals?'

George nodded. 'That's right. I think that's what Sam was worried about most. She knows more than she's said. Probably too scared even to think about it, never mind describe it. Bullets and bombs just kill you, but some of that stuff will pass down through the generations, killing people who haven't even been born yet. There's a heap of chemical weapons stored in there, in amongst the guns and missiles, and the ammo.'

'Anything you recognized from the codes?'

'Yes, unfortunately. One thing's for sure. The US Army sure didn't store it all together like that. There's no way trained logistics and ordnance people would do that.'

'Probably Viktor's people, then,' John said thoughtfully. 'That what you're thinking?'

'I am. For the US Army, supply depots are one thing, and ammunition dumps another. You don't combine the two.

'Dumps are extremely hazardous places that blow sky high sometimes for no good reason at all. They always have been. Even in the days of cannon and muskets the powder magazines were kept well away from everything else.

'As for chemical weapons,' George added heavily, 'they don't bear thinking about, even when they are isolated — especially the unitary weapons.'

'They're the ones that don't need different chemicals mixing together?'

'Darned right! They're the ones ready to go, once you open the barrel. Part of the family known as "Weapons of Mass Destruction".'

'I thought those things were banned.'

'They are — all of 'em, not just the unitaries. The Chemical Weapons Convention of 1993 created a legally binding, world-wide ban on the production, stockpiling and use of chemical weapons. Blah-blah-blah.

'The trouble is that a lot of countries had big stockpiles, and it's taking thirty years to get rid of them. That's just the ones that are known about! The US's stockpile will be gone by 2019, and Russia's a year later, supposedly.'

'But you don't think so?'

'Well . . . you saw what was in there, didn't you, even if you didn't recognize all of it?'

John nodded. 'What did you see, George?'

The other man sighed and reached out his cup. 'Any coffee left in that flask?'

'Some,' John said, shaking the flask and listening. He removed the stopper and poured him another half-cupful. 'We should brew some more. So what did you see, George?'

'I saw pallets of artillery shells. Some were labelled HN. That's Nitrogen Mustard, a blister agent. I saw GB, Sarin. And GF, Cyclosarin. They're both nerve agents. Then there were some pulmonary agents to destroy your lungs: CG, which is Phosphene, and CI, which is Chlorine. That enough for you?'

John grimaced. 'More than enough.'

'We have to get rid of it, kid.'

'Because if we don't . . . ?'

'Someone, somewhere, will use it eventually.'

John nodded. 'Agreed. Can it be destroyed, though? Can we do it?'

'Well, incineration is the usual method. The US has got rid of a lot that way, in depots from Alabama to Utah, and even on the Johnson Atoll in the Pacific.'

John thought about it a moment and then said, 'That fits in nicely with what I was thinking of doing. One thing, though. What will your bosses in Washington say?'

George shrugged. 'Not my bosses any more. Officially, I'm retired. I'm doing this job for an old friend — the guy that's no longer with us. Jack Olsson. He would approve and cheer us on. I'm sure of that. The rest of 'em don't count, so far as I'm concerned.'

'You sure?'

'I'm sure.'

They were quiet for a minute or two. Then John said, 'Why do you suppose the US Army set that place up?'

'Oh, they've got depots and ammunition dumps all over the world — anywhere where US interests might need protection, either now or in future.

'The military will have set it up. Then, my guess is they paid Sirko a whole lot of money to look after it, on condition of strict secrecy. It's a forward base. Probably they expected Ukraine to flare up before it actually did.'

'There would need to have been government connivance for that to happen, surely?'

'Oh, sure. And at certain times, depending on who was currently the President, that would have been forthcoming readily enough. Yulia Tymoshenko would have been happy enough to see it done. Probably Yushchenko before her, too. They'd had enough of Russia.'

They brooded over that for a little while. Then George added, 'Something else we need to consider, John.'

'What's that?'

'Amongst all that stuff in there, some of it isn't US ordnance.'

'No? What else did you see?'

'Some of them crates contain missiles made in Russia.'

'Like the one that brought down the Malaysian plane the other year?'

'Exactly.'

'Oh, shit!'

'Still, that's not the truly bad stuff. The chemicals are the worst. Enough to poison a large part of Europe if they ever get used. And that's just counting the codes I know.'

'We really do have to get rid of it.' John grimaced. 'What the hell was Viktor doing, storing that stuff?'

164

'Maybe it wasn't his fault. He would have been just told to store what he was given. He wouldn't even know what some of it was, let alone what it can do.'

John nodded. 'You're probably right. Viktor was no more familiar with ordnance codes than I am. I'm sure of that.'

'But Jack Olsson was.'

'What was his role?'

'I don't know if he had one, not for sure. But he was certainly some sort of channel between Sirko and Washington. He'll have known something of what was going on here.

'I wouldn't be surprised if part of his role was to keep a watch on this place, and make sure Sirko was looking after it properly, and nothing was being filched.'

'I thought he was an arms salesman.'

'Not as such, although that might have come into it.' George shrugged. 'But his job was to do whatever he was told to do. That was true for all of us, ultimately.'

'So who would have been responsible for the depot — back in Washington, I mean? Somebody must have been.'

George shrugged. 'My boss? The US Army? The cloud, maybe? I'm fucked if I know!'

'And what were they thinking, I wonder. What was the point of it?'

'Contingency planning, I expect. If the Russians had chemical weapons, which they certainly did, we'll have wanted the Ukrainians to have them too — and we'll have let the Russians know they did. That way, there would be less chance of them being used.'

'Takes you back to the MAD days, doesn't it?'

'Mutual Assured Destruction.' George nodded. 'It sure does.'

'So what are we going to do?'

George thought for a moment and then said, 'Make sure them things get used on nobody — ever!'

'Good.' John nodded with approval. 'And I think I know how we can do that.'

'Before we get to that, though, John, there's one or two other things I'd like to take care of first.'

'Oh?'

'There's Yugov, for one. Then there's who set him on to you.'

'The leak in Washington, you're thinking about?'

George nodded.

'Any ideas about that?'

'Some,' George said, nodding again.

CHAPTER THIRTY-EIGHT

George Riley was troubled. The chemical weapons were one thing, a very serious thing, but in some ways he was more troubled by what was going on generally. Yugov's involvement was part of it. How had that happened? There had to have been a leak. Somebody, somewhere, had told Yugov something. Somebody in Washington? Increasingly, he thought that pretty likely.

It could have been somebody in Slovakia, but when Olsson's body was returned to the US authorities, the Slovaks couldn't have known whose body it was. Just an American citizen, so far as they were concerned. A body to get rid of after ten years.

Besides, the Slovaks couldn't have known about the depot in Ukraine. Surely not? Even if they had got wind of it, they couldn't possibly have known exactly where it was, or of Sirko's involvement. No one outside of Washington could have put all that together. Even in Washington, there wouldn't have been many in the intelligence community who knew what was going on. Hardly any at all, in fact.

As for the guys who created and built the depot, they did it but they wouldn't have known where the hell they were when they were doing it. Just another depot, somewhere in Eurasia. Flown in at night, and lifted back out again on another night when the job was done. They would have known it wasn't Africa, but not much more than that. Its location would have had to be kept secret.

Special Forces people, even the back-up guys who handled logistics, were used to that kind of secrecy. It wouldn't have bothered them. Hell, they'd created much bigger bases than that all over the Asian republics of the former Soviet Union without knowing much about where they were. Give 'em a job to do, and they got on and did it. That's how it was.

No, it had to be Washington where the leak had sprung. So he'd better talk to Ted Pearson again.

'How's it going, George?'

'About the same as last time we spoke, Ted. But I'm afraid one or two of Yugov's guys didn't make it.'

'That's a real shame, George. How about Yugov himself?'

'Oh, he made sure he got out in good time. I'm not sure where he is right now.'

'And Tait?'

'Still around. He says he didn't take Olsson down, and I believe him.'

'Well, he would say that, wouldn't he? Follow the evidence, George. That's all I can say.'

'Yeah. I'm still thinking there's a leak back there in DC. How else could Yugov have homed in on Tait?'

'Who knows, George? A guy like him will have paid informers everywhere, even in Slovakia, I wouldn't be surprised. That's probably where you need to look, George, not back here. I haven't seen or heard anything to justify your suspicion. I'll keep looking, of course.'

Of course, George thought. Of course you will. But your heart's not in it, is it? I can tell that.

'Ted, you ever hear anything about an arms depot Sirko was involved with, a secret arms depot?'

'Where? In Ukraine?'

'Yeah.'

There was a long pause before Pearson answered. 'Just wracking my brains here, George. There was something, back then. Difficult to recall the details, but we did build one some-where, I believe. Hell, we built them things all over the god-damn place! Kazakhstan, Uzbekistan, and all the rest of the Stans, as well. Ukraine and Poland, too, I wouldn't be surprised. Why do you ask?'

George was equivocal, not wanting to admit to too much. 'Tait said something. It made me wonder.'

'I'll look into it. See if you can find anything more from him. Knowing the location would help. I could take a look out there myself. Might be interesting.'

'Yeah. Right. I'll see what he knows. One more thing, Ted. Just why would Yugov be interested in something like that? Any ideas?'

'Well, Yugov got burned in the east, where all this conflict is going on. That might have something to do with it. A lot of the factories and works he took over from Sirko have been obliterated in the fighting, I believe. So I guess he must be looking for ways to find compensation. The money Tait took from Olsson would be a help, if he could get it, wouldn't it?'

'Yeah. If it's still around, I'll find it.'

'Take care, George. Don't go out on a limb for a couple of million bucks, not at this time of life.'

Sonofabitch, that was an odd concluding remark, George thought afterwards. A couple of million bucks, when he knew the number was ten? In fact, the whole damned conversation had been odd. He was beginning to wonder if Ted knew more than he had said, a lot more. Well, of course he did. It was his job.

All the same, it rankled that Ted had held back on him. Having coaxed him out of retirement, on what was essentially an old pals together act, he should have been more forthcom-ing with him. The depot, for example. Of course he knew about it. There was no doubt about that. He seemed to know a lot about Yugov's current financial circumstances, as well. Was that just guesswork?

As for Tait, well, he was beginning to wonder if Ted had known all along that Tait wasn't the man who had killed Jack Olsson. He hadn't been surprised by anything he had told him. In which case, he thought sourly, what the hell am I doing here — or in England, where I'm supposed to be?

Perhaps Ted knew who Tait's wife was, as well? Maybe that was even the reason he had sent him to England, to see what he could find out about her, after he'd decided Tait wasn't Olsson's killer? Hell, anything was possible. There was nothing new about the operative on the ground being given only part of the story. He'd just forgotten how it was always like that. Chopping firewood in his own back yard had slowed him down. Made him sentimental about the old times. Maybe Ted had even been counting on that.

If all this was true, though, if Ted really had told him only part of the story deliberately, the question was why? What game was he playing? What was he really after?

Something was going on. That much was clear. Something had made dragging an old warhorse like himself back out of retirement seem a good idea. He wondered what it could be.

Then he grimaced as he thought about it realistically, objectively. One good possible reason was that whatever Ted was up to, he wanted full deniability if it went wrong. How better than to use a retired operative who was no longer on the department's books? Surely not? Well, Ted was capable of it. He knew that from old.

Mind you, he thought with a wry smile, he was nearly as bad himself. Why hadn't he told Ted more about the depot? And why hadn't he mentioned that he was here in Ukraine, right now?

Natural caution and self-defence, he told himself bleakly. Experience. A gut feeling. And the old rules applied still. You never had been able to trust anyone in this game.

Having said that, he also wondered if Ted already knew where he was. Maybe he had somebody keeping tabs on his sat phone? That, too, would be natural, and so would be not admitting as much.

CHAPTER THIRTY-NINE

They decided to crack on with their plans for the depot. Early next morning they left the room in a village some miles away from where they had stayed overnight. They headed back to the cave, to see what explosives were available. There was no shortage.

'This may be more your game than mine,' George suggested. 'Guns, yes. But I've not had a lot to do with explosives.'

'Well, it's been a while,' John said with a wry grin. 'These days, I build things up instead of knocking them down. But I'll see what I can do. Hopefully, things haven't changed too much.'

The crates of explosives were all in one section of the depot.

'Sweet Jesus!' George said, wincing as he scanned the racks. 'What were they thinking, the guys that piled all this stuff here?'

'Not health and safety,' John said grimly. 'We can be sure of that. But it'll make things easier for us — if it doesn't blow before we're done.'

'What are we looking for?' George asked as John ranged along the stacks. 'Anything in particular? There's enough here to blow up half of Europe!'

'Bear with me, George. I'll know it when I see it.'

'Lots of C4, I see. That's what the US Army likes. Not to mention the SEALs, and probably the rest of the military.'

John shook his head. 'I wasn't trained to use that stuff. So I don't much like it. I'm looking for something I'm familiar with.'

It didn't take them much longer.

'Ah! Here's what I want — Semtex.'

They had stopped before a stack of pallets holding containers marked with the usual emblems: skull and crossbones, fire hazard, flammable, etc. And helpfully labelled *Semtex-10*.

'Here it is!' John said with satisfaction. 'This is the version they've been producing since 1987.'

'The old Czechoslovak stuff, eh?' George mused.

'You're right. It is old. First manufactured in the early 1960s, but I seriously doubt if anybody has come up with anything better yet — if you want things that reliably go bang but are safe until they're set up.'

They worked quickly, John deciding where best to place the plastic charges, and George helping him move and position them. Then they collected some reels of detonating cord and started carefully stringing them all together. The aim, and the hope, was that the det cord would ensure a simultaneous explosion from all the charges.

It was demanding work, and it took time. Despite the sub-zero temperature outside, inside the cave they were soon sweating heavily.

'One thing's for sure,' John said after a while. 'When this lot goes up, there'll be plenty of fuel for the flames. There won't be any doubt about how effective the incineration is.'

George straightened up for a moment and looked around. 'Gives me the creeps, this place. I won't be sorry to see the back of it.'

'Oh, it's your neat and tidy instinct coming to the fore. You just don't like seeing explosives and bullets all mixed up with chemicals and trucks and stuff. Offends your sense of propriety and order.'

'Damn right,' George grunted. 'I'd like to hear what a quartermaster would have to say about it. He'd blast our ears off.'

'Well, with a bit of luck, no one like that is going to have to give an opinion.'

The work took all day, and it was a hard day's work. As well as the physical labour, there was a lot of thinking and working out mentally to do. John didn't bother about calculating the size of the charges. They were not short of explosives and he jammed stuff together extravagantly. They wanted, needed, a very big bang, and then a raging inferno. With this lot, he thought grimly, there was little danger of falling short.

More tricky was rigging a fuse system. They had to have a safe detonation, when they were well away from the site — a very long way, given the nature of the cave's contents. Using mobile phones seemed the best bet.

He opted to detonate the blasting cap by using one of their mobile phones to phone a modified phone that they would leave at the entrance to the cave system. In turn, that would fire off the det cord. And that would set off a chain leading to the very big bang and raging inferno they required. That was the theory.

George nodded approvingly, and with interest. 'I did wonder how we could trigger the blast, yet be far enough away to be out of harm's way. Cell phones, eh? You know how to do it?'

'If I can remember,' John said tersely. 'It's been a while.'

'There won't be any reception inside the cave, but you've figured that out, haven't you?'

'Yep. We'll leave the trigger outside, and start the chain there.'

'You're a smart guy, Tait.'

John shook his head. 'If I was smart, I would never have got involved with this stuff in the first place. I wouldn't be here now, either.'

'True enough,' George said ruefully. 'I've often thought that myself.'

'It's ready to go,' John said wearily at last.

'OK. That's good. But we're not going to blow it yet.'

'No?'

'Let's leave it for now. We'll fire it off soon, but first we need to talk, and I need to make a phone call or two.'

John stared at him for a moment and shook his head. 'You're looking to do more than just blow this lot up, aren't you?'

'Damned right,' George said. 'Before we do that, we need to find out what's been going on — and who's been responsible for it.'

CHAPTER FORTY

Back at the vehicle, they warmed up some soup on a little gas stove they had picked up in Kiev, along with some other camping gear. They tore apart a loaf of rye bread and a length of salami. Boiled a kettle of water to make coffee, and refill the flask.

'We should have bought a tent, as well,' John said.

'Don't need a tent. The SUV's good enough.'

'One tent for you, and another for me. That would have been better. You can't hear somebody snoring through tent walls, can you?' John said with a grin.

'That your problem, huh?'

'Not mine. It's yours.'

'It shouldn't bother you tonight, not after a day's work like we've just done.'

'True enough.'

They sat in the vehicle with the doors closed. It was cold out there, and getting colder. The ground was frozen hard and covered with a fresh dusting of snow.

'Maybe more snow to come tonight,' George said, wiping a clear patch on the windscreen so he could look up at the sky.

'You'll feel it in your bones, eh, an old hunter like you?'

'That's right. I do. I wouldn't have taken kindly to sleeping on the ground tonight. Feel grateful we've got this nice big, warm vehicle, and those nice big, fluffy sleeping bags.'

'Yeah. I do. I'm grateful.'

John gazed out into the blackness all around them. He was restless, impatient, eager to get on with it. He resented the delay. They could have finished the job and been out of here tonight. Across the border, like last time he was in this country. Or back at the airport, ready to board a plane to London. They could have been out of here, the damned cave blown to smithereens. Instead, they still had it all to do. He wasn't best suited.

'Tell me again, George, why we're stuck here in this godforsaken spot that maybe is very pleasant in summer but right now is the shits. Remind me. I seem to have forgotten the rationale. Just tell me why we're sleeping in this fucking car tonight!'

George chuckled. 'You young fellas! No staying power, have you? No patience. No memory!'

John grinned reluctantly.

'It's not that. I just don't have your training and your experience of Machiavellian thought processes. I was a soldier once — not a bloody assassin! And even that was a long time ago. Mostly now I'm a builder. Or I was, until you and Yugov arrived on the scene. I'm kidding,' he added. 'Don't mind me. I'm just sounding off. Thinking we could have been out of here, job done, and on the way home by now.'

'Not really done,' George said slowly, patiently. 'Yugov would still be out there somewhere, remember? You and your wife would still be at risk from him. And someone back in Washington would still be lining his pockets.'

'That what you think is happening?'

'I'm not sure. I need to talk to Ted again.'

'Your boss?'

'Used to be all the time. Now he is just for this one job.'

'Which was supposed to be shooting me?'

George nodded. 'And might be again,' he warned, 'if you don't stop bitching!'

Laughing, John said, 'Maybe he's been doing the leaking?'

'Ted? Yeah. It's possible. I don't like the idea, though. Ted and me go back a long, long way. But I need to check.'

'How?'

'I've been thinking about that a lot. I had to do something to distract me while we were in that damned cave. I decided the quickest way to do it, and satisfy myself one way or the other, is to tell Ted the precise location of the depot.'

After a stunned pause for thought, John said, 'How the hell would that work?'

'Simple. If nobody arrives here in the next twenty-four hours — or maybe a bit longer — Ted has nothing to do with the leaking. If somebody arrives here hotfoot, well, then, the story is different.'

'So when do we blow the cave? Do we blow it at all?'

'Oh, yes. There's no doubt about that. We're gonna blow her sky high. Ain't nobody going to get their hands on them chemical weapons.'

'A lot of good stuff, useful stuff, is going to go with them.'

'Yeah. But there's a price to be paid for everything. I'm sure the people of Ukraine — whichever side they're on in this battle in the east — will thank us for sparing them what's happened in certain places in Iraq and Syria.'

True enough, John was thinking. They would survive another Russian occupation, if it came to that. Maybe even in the long run all would be forgiven, if not forgotten. But huge numbers of people would not survive the release of the contents of that cave. And many more would suffer the effects of it for the rest of their miserable lives, as would their children and grandchildren.

'Better get on the phone, George,' he said gruffly.

George mulled it over a few more minutes before he dug out his phone and made the call.

'Out on the golf course, Ted?'

There was a wry chuckle at the other end. 'I should be. Maybe I would be doing myself more good. How's it going over there, George?'

'Good, Ted. Real good. I've got some information for you about that depot at last. Remember we talked about it?'

'Oh, yeah. Great. I could do with some good news. So what you got?'

'Got pen and paper handy? I'm going to give you the coordinates.'

'One moment. Right. Go ahead.'

George read out the sequence of twelve digits taken from his GPS.

'That's great. Thanks, George. It beggars belief that we have no record of this depot, but there it is.'

'How did that happen, do you suppose?'

'It was off the books, George. Secret, secret. Viktor Sirko was commissioned to manage it, and we relied on him to do it well.'

He didn't do it too well, George thought. All that dangerous stuff jammed in together? A nightmare!

'What will be in it, Ted? Anything special?'

'Just the usual. Supplies. Equipment. Weapons. Why do you ask?'

'Just wondering if there's likely to be anything dangerous there, anything real nasty.'

There was a pause. Then Ted said suspiciously, 'Where are you, George?'

'The same place.'

After a significant pause, Ted said, 'Oh, yeah. I see that now. The Northumberland place. Still looking for Olsson's killer?'

'Still looking.'

'Keep looking, George. Meanwhile, I'll see to it that the people who count in Ukraine get this information. The contents of that depot will be important to them. They're desperately short of the armaments they need to stop the Russian advance in the east, and we can't send them anything at all.'

'That bad, huh?'

'Damn right. The President doesn't want to upset our wonderful allies in Europe, who all want to continue with the diplomatic arts, while Ukrainian boys are getting blown away by weapons they can't match. We've lost our bottle, as the Brits say. We don't want to escalate this thing with Russia. Putin is laughing at us!'

'I heard he said he could have troops in Warsaw, Prague and everywhere else in a fortnight, if he chose to.'

'I tell you, George. We're running scared. Until we get a new president, Putin can do whatever the hell he likes. We won't even try to stop him.

'But maybe this depot will help our allies on the ground a little bit. I'd like to arrange for that before I take my leave of this town, and shuffle off out of here.

'And you've done your bit, George. I thank you. All that's left for you to do now is settle with Jack Olsson's killer. Then we're both done.'

CHAPTER FORTY-ONE

There was a period of silence after George switched off his phone. A flurry of snow pattered against the windscreen. The car rocked a little.

'Wind's getting up,' George remarked at last.

John nodded. 'Could be a cold night. I just hope we don't get a lot of snow overnight. It could complicate things.'

'The charge?'

'Yeah. I was thinking of adding a fuse to the detonator, as back-up in case the phone doesn't work.'

'It's well protected, isn't it?'

John grimaced. 'It should be all right. And it wouldn't be hard to hide our tracks if we did go back.'

'Well, we don't need to go back for any other reason. How likely is it that the phone won't work?'

John shrugged. 'No idea. The cold could be a problem, but I don't really know. Whatever we do, or don't do, it will be a gamble.'

George thought about it. 'Leave it,' he said. 'We'll take the risk.'

That said, and tacitly agreed, John waited a moment before saying, 'This Ted, your boss. He thinks you're still back in Northumberland?'

'Yeah. I thought he might monitor the signal on the phone he gave me to use. I didn't want that. So I left it back there. As I suspected he might do, he checked.'

You wily old devil! John thought with amusement. That's what came from a lifetime of experience, he supposed.

'So what do you think now, having spoken to him?'

George gave a heavy sigh and straightened up in his seat. 'I don't think Ted's after the Olsson money — or any other money, if it comes to that. He'll have enough already to fund his retirement. I don't believe he's a real greedy guy.

'But I don't know yet if he was the leak. If he was, it will be because he's sick and tired of watching the Russian aggression in eastern Ukraine go unanswered. He wants the contents of that depot released to the Ukrainians. He wants to help them, but he can't go against the President, the Congress, and everyone else in official Washington. This is a way around that embargo. He wants to take it.'

'I'm not sure where that leaves us,' John said reflectively.

'Out in the cold!' George chuckled without sounding amused. 'I don't know about you, son, but if anyone gets their hands on what's in that cave, I wouldn't trust them not to use it. If they don't use it themselves, they'll sell or pass it on to someone who will.'

'That sounds about right.' John sighed wearily. 'I liked this country, the time I spent here. Hell, it's my wife's homeland! So lily-livered though it might sound, I would rather see it back under Russian occupation than devastated by chemical weapons.'

'Me, too. I've seen up close how those things work.'

'So we're in agreement — we're still going to blow the damned thing up?'

'You bet,' George said. 'But first let's see if anyone turns up here. Let's see if Ted is the leak.'

'How long do we give it? A couple of days?'

'Or until the food runs out,' George said wryly. 'I'm not sure this is good hunting country.'

'Oh, it is!' John assured him. 'But your snoring is likely to get me down if we have to wait longer than a couple of days.'

CHAPTER FORTY-TWO

It was a hard night. They were warm enough in their sleeping bags inside the car, but the wind howled and the snow flew all night long, shaking and rattling them constantly. In the morning the storm had passed on, leaving a fresh, white world.

They struggled out and got themselves moving early. After a cup of coffee and more bread and salami, they set off, heading up on to the ridge overlooking the vicinity of the cave. It was hard going in knee-deep snow. As the younger and stronger man, John took the lead by unspoken agreement and broke trail. George made use of the footprints he left behind.

Leaving evidence of their passing didn't matter, as they were approaching the ridge overlooking the Dniester valley, and the vicinity of the cave, from the far side of the low range of hills. The plan was to go nowhere near the cave. Up on the ridge, they would be a good half mile away. John just hoped they didn't freeze to death while they were waiting to see if anyone came. A few hours would be all right, but they couldn't spend a night up there.

The prospect didn't seem to worry his companion. Tough old bugger, George, he thought with a wry smile. No doubt, as a sniper, he'd done plenty of waiting in his time.

Not always in comfort, either. And he was a hunter. So he would have inner resources of fortitude and resilience to call upon when needed. He'd better have, John thought grimly. They had let themselves in for a challenging vigil.

It was bitterly cold up on the hills. Heads down against a rising wind that hadn't been apparent at lower levels, they soldiered on, tramping their way towards the crest of the ridge. Fortunately, the snow wasn't so deep higher up, which helped them make better progress.

John paused when they reached the ridge. George drew level with him and they looked down on the copse of woodland close to the cave entrance.

'Around here would be good,' John suggested, squinting against the icy wind as he turned to face his companion.

George nodded. 'We're close enough, and we've got a good view. We need to get down out of this wind, though.'

He pointed downslope a dozen feet, or so. 'Let's dig in down there. No need to stay up here.'

It made sense. John led the way down to the spot George had pointed out. Off the summit ridge, they were sheltered from the wind, and digging into the snow patch gave them even greater protection from it. They both knew, too, that packed in snow they would suffer less body heat loss.

'I don't know how long we'll be able to last out,' George said, 'but we'll give it a go. Better keep an eye on each other, and check every half hour for signs of frostbite or hypothermia.'

John nodded. 'Like you, George, I've done this sort of thing before — but a while ago now.'

'Where was that?'

'You don't want to know. You don't need to know!'

'Arctic Norway?'

'There as well.'

George chuckled. 'They once had me stationed over in Poland, close to the Russian border.'

'Could have been worse. You could have been guarding the Aleutian islands, in case some Ruskies tried to slip across from Siberia to Alaska.'

'Don't I know it. Fortunately, they didn't think they needed a sniper there.'

'That what you were?'

'Yeah. But not an army sniper. I was better than that. More specialized. More of a hitman.'

'Good to have you along, in that case!'

They took turns to watch the target area. A half hour observing; then a half hour resting and doing exercises in the snow hole, to keep the blood circulating. At all times they did their best to keep the weapons they had taken from the depot under their coats to protect them from the cold. Without speaking about it, they knew there might come a time when they needed to shoot somebody.

By eight it was as light as it was going to get beneath a cloudy sky that seemed to have plenty more snow left in it. John had just done a shift. Now it was up to George to watch out for movement down below.

Nothing happened.

John took over again a half hour later, and then George from him once more. Neither of them had seen anything alive and moving by ten.

While he was doing some more exercises, John said, 'How are you doing, old timer?'

George chuckled through chapped lips. 'Just wishing I was back on that moor above your house, young fella. It was warmer there.'

'Too true. We nearly drowned, but at least we were warm — most of the time.'

John was tired of stretching hands and arms, feet and knees. Tired of deep breathing through the sleeve of his coat. Wondering if they were making a big mistake, sitting up here, he wished more strongly than ever that they had just blown the cave and quit.

'Don't say it!' George cautioned.

'What?'

'You know — and I know. Just keep it under your breath. We're not blowing the cave yet. We've got to give it more time.'

But how much longer? They were going to die, sitting up here.

'Let me look at your face, George. It's my turn coming up, but I want to see how you're doing before I take over from you.'

'I'm doing OK. Nothing about this that I can't handle.'

'No, of course there isn't. Let me look at your damned face!'

George acquiesced. John looked. There were no bad signs yet. No white patches or blue lips. No black areas under the skin foretelling of gangrene, thank God!

'Now your hands.'

He tested George's fingers for stiffness.

'We're going to have to watch it. You've not got as much movement as you should have. Probably the same for me, as well.'

'It's just the damn gloves.'

'Maybe. What about your feet? How are they?'

'I can still feel 'em, if that's what you mean.'

'That's a good sign!' John chuckled. 'They haven't dropped off yet. But we really will have to watch it. We're not generating any heat at all, sitting here like this.'

'It's nothing I've not done plenty of before.'

'No, of course it isn't, you being such a terrific hunter and sniper, and general outdoors man, and all.'

'I wish I'd never told you now,' George said, managing to raise a chuckle.

'Tell you what, though. By late afternoon we should quit. We can't survive a night out here.'

Maybe not even the rest of the day, he thought to himself. And I'm in no better shape than he is. My feet are aching with the cold, and there's damn all I can do about it, apart from getting on them and starting to walk.

'Let's just see how it goes,' George suggested.

'Yeah.'

The day slowed down. The half hours spent with their heads far enough up to see down into the valley grew longer, interminably so. And nothing happened. Nothing at all. Still. Once, John thought he saw a bird flying by, but when he focused his eyes better there was nothing there. Nothing at all. Just white, everywhere.

Nothing happened, again and again. They continued swapping places. From time to time, they chewed salami and bread, and sipped coffee from the big flask they had brought with them. The cold induced fatigue, a bone-chilling weariness that glazed the mind and stilled restless limbs agitating to try to create heat.

It seemed as if nothing would happen, ever.

But just after three in the afternoon they came.

CHAPTER FORTY-THREE

John saw them first. Three pick-up trucks appeared down by the frozen river far below. They were the first vehicles they had seen all day. The trucks stopped briefly, as if for consultation, and then began to wind their way up the rough forestry track below the cave.

'They're here!' he said tersely. 'Somebody is.'

He reached for the field glasses under his coat. George came up out of the snow hole alongside him. John handed him the glasses after taking a quick look himself.

'A reconnaissance party,' George said gruffly.

'Yeah.'

By the time the pick-ups had parked close to the cave, a convoy of much bigger trucks had arrived on the riverside road.

'Looks like they mean business,' George said.

John nodded. He was waiting to see who the new arrivals were, but already it looked as though the trap had worked.

'Ted got the word out to these guys pretty fast,' George remarked. 'They haven't wasted any time either.'

Several men got out of the pick-ups to confer. George focused the glasses and swore.

'What?' John demanded.

'Yugov. Now we know everything,' he added bitterly. 'Fucking Ted!'

He handed the glasses over. John studied the group of figures and confirmed the identity of Yugov. He gave the glasses back and sank down into the snow hole.

'You've got your answer, George. It was a leak, and now we know who's been doing it,' he said hoarsely. 'Let's blow the cave.'

George shook his head and stayed where he was, watching still.

John hugged himself, trying to get more warmth into his frozen body. He had no idea how the older man was feeling but he was fucking frozen himself. To hell with this shit! He'd had enough.

'Come on George, for chrissake! Let's blow the fucking thing, and get the hell out of here.'

'Another vehicle has arrived,' George said, ignoring him. 'Another truck with a double cab. It's come right up to join the others. Holy shit!'

'What now?' John sprang back up.

'It's Ted Pearson!'

'You're kidding? Here, give me the glasses.'

George handed them over and leant back, putting his palms over his eyes to try to warm them. John focused and saw a tall, very upright older guy talking to Yugov.

'The big bloke?'

'Yeah. That's Ted. What the hell is he doing here?'

'They're old pals, it looks like. Shaking hands and kissing each other. It makes me feel sick.'

'That's Ted. Always was a great party mingler.'

'How the hell has he got here so fast?' John demanded, turning to look at the other man.

'There's only one explanation I can think of — he was here all along.'

George sank back into the snow hole and fumbled under his clothing.

John stayed where he was, watching the scene play out down below. 'What are you doing?'

'Calling him,' George said tersely.

'What the hell for?'

'We've got to be sure. I'll put it on loud speaker, so you can hear it.'

John shook his head. He was close to despair. He had no idea where they were going with this now.

George was near despair, too, but for a different reason. He was wondering to what extent he'd been suckered all along.

'He's getting his phone out!' John snapped, watching as Ted Pearson moved aside from the group.

George just nodded. He was concentrating on how to handle this.

'That you, George?'

'Hi, Ted! How are you doing?'

'The same as last time we spoke. What can I do for you, George?'

'I've got some news for you. That depot in Ukraine? I've been talking to Tait's wife about it again.'

'Yeah? Ask her about the key. Where is it? She seems to be the only one who knows, since Sirko and his crew got themselves killed.'

'It's open already, she says. She wasn't going to be the only person who knew about it. So she had it opened up.'

'Oh? That's good news. I'm actually intending to visit Ukraine myself. I'll take some guys with me to look it over.'

'Ted, Vlasta Sirko says not to go in there. She says the depot's full of toxic stuff — chemical weapons, and a whole lot of other things that are not very nice.'

'The Ukrainians need those weapons, George. If they're going to have a chance of stopping the Russians, they have to have them. There's nothing coming to them from the US, or anywhere else in the West.'

'They should stay where they are, in my opinion. And what about Yugov? Where does he fit into all this?'

'Yugov? Oh, you don't need to worry about him any-more. He's with me, George. I'm using him, employing him. He's going to get the stuff out of the depot and put it in the right hands. There's nobody else who can do that, without the US — and me! — taking the blame.'

'Ted, for chrissake!' George said angrily. 'Tell me you're not paying Yugov?'

'He's a businessman, George. And I need him. We need each other. He's lost a lot of factories in the fighting in the east, and needs to rebuild his business. And I need his distri-bution network.'

'He's a killer, Ted. It was him that had Jack Olsson whacked. Remember Jack — and why you brought me out of retirement?'

'This is more important. Right now, he's an ally.'

'Don't do this, Ted. You don't need to do this.'

'I've been working on this project with Yugov for quite a while, George. You need to know that. I'm not going to stop now. We're doing what's right.'

George paused for a moment. Then he said, 'Keep out of the damned cave, Ted. Don't you or Yugov dare touch anything in there.'

'Come on, George, for chrissake! Do you think I'm going to let the goddamn Russians walk all over yet another country? We've been fighting them all our lives, one way or another. Come and join us!'

'The stuff in there's too dangerous ever to be brought out.'

'Crap! The Ukrainians will be glad to have it. It's a bit one-sided at the moment. We're going to even things up a little.'

'Make things worse, you mean!' George said bitterly. 'That's the old better-dead-than-red song sheet you're read-ing from, Ted. Them days are over.'

'Get real, George.'

'He's ended the call,' George said in disbelief.

'It wasn't going anywhere,' John said. 'You were wasting your breath. What were you doing, trying to save his miserable skin?'

George slumped down into the snow hole again and sat for a while with his thoughts.

John let him be. Something was going on in the other man's head that he didn't want to intrude on. Instead, he watched as a party down below brought the first consignment of weapons out of the cave. A big truck was making its way up the track, to receive it.

'They're moving stuff out already,' he said tersely. 'They've started.'

George didn't reply.

First it would be small stuff, rifles and ammunition. Then there would be armoured vehicles, missiles — and the rest of it. John felt himself tensing with the weight of expectation. Come on, George! he said under his breath. For chrissake, make up your mind!

George moved up alongside him. They watched as Yugov and Pearson conferred, spoke to a group of Yugov's men and then walked into the cave entrance together. They were going to see for themselves.

John steeled himself to be controlled, unwilling to make the decision. This was George's call.

The seconds passed. A couple of minutes went by. No one had emerged from the cave yet. The big truck labouring up the track had almost reached the pick-ups.

'Make the call,' George snapped.

John took out his phone and began to tap in the sequence of digits.

CHAPTER FORTY-FOUR

For long moments nothing happened. They waited and watched in silence. George turned his head slightly to look at John, who grimaced and bared his teeth in anguish.

He didn't know. He just didn't know. Maybe he hadn't got it right. There were never any guarantees it would work anyway. The cold . . .

Then it started.

It began as a slow rumble they felt rather than heard. Snow on the slope in front of them began to slide. Far below, a trace of smoke appeared in the cave entrance. Puffs of it appeared elsewhere. The world began to shiver and became hazy. Then the surface of the land below seemed to shudder violently. Masses of snow and frozen rock began to rise slowly from the surface of the ground, reaching up into the sky.

'Down!' John snapped, grabbing George by the shoulders and pulling him backwards.

They both slid down into the snow hole, cowering there and listening with awe as shock waves blasted over their heads and a roaring noise passed them by like a mighty avalanche. The atmospheric disturbance was followed moments later by the muffled thunder of a huge explosion somewhere beneath the earth itself, and the air over their heads filled with flying debris.

Lumps of rock, boulders and showers of gravel, ice and snow rained down on them for several minutes. They closed their eyes, protected their heads with their arms and made themselves small. They stayed where they were, in a state of shock and disbelief for what seemed like an eternity.

Eventually, it all stopped. At last, John opened his eyes and said in a hoarse voice, 'It's over.'

'Thank God!' George said in a strained voice. 'That was a helluva bang you engineered for us, son.'

'The best I've ever done,' John replied, with an attempt at a grin that felt as if it was cracking his face open. 'Better take a look.'

He scrambled upright and peered downslope. The landscape had changed. The ground below their position was no longer pristine white with new snow. Now it was a dirty colour, covered by muck and filth from the explosion. Black smoke, pouring now from a variety of fissures, cracks and holes, indicated there were fires raging deep below the surface.

The big truck they had watched labouring up the slope towards the entrance to the cave was no longer where it had been, although a pile of burning wreckage some distance away indicated where what was left of it might be located now. The four pick-ups that had brought Yugov and Pearson, and the others, had simply disappeared. It looked as though the other big trucks alongside the river had also been hit and badly damaged. Two were smoking. One had a strangely crumpled appearance. Another lay twisted across the road.

After a long, searching look, George nodded, turned his head and said, 'That takes care of business. We'd better get out of here while we still can.'

John agreed and started to clamber out of the snow hole that had been their refuge for the past many hours, scarcely able to believe how cold and stiff he was and feeling relieved he was still capable of moving at all. He gave George his hand and helped him out, too. Then, without a backward glance, they set off back to the car.

Already, John noted, it was growing dark, but at least the wind had died down now, as if shocked by what had happened down by the river.

The way back was downhill most of the way on long, gentle slopes, and the easier for it, but in the eerie light of a gathering winter night under a starlit sky, it was as strange a journey as John could remember. Silent, mostly. They didn't talk. They seemed to have arrived at an unspoken consensus that there was nothing worth saying.

He didn't dwell on the mayhem behind them. That was for another day. For a while, he took refuge in the knowledge of the chaos they had averted by what they had done. It was a comfort.

But he didn't even think very much about that, either. Mostly, he focused on putting one foot in front of the other, and making sure that George was able to do the same. He wasn't as fit and durable himself as he had once been, but the older man was of a different generation altogether. They had had some hard days, and now they couldn't afford a catastrophic slip and injury on these icy slopes. They had to leave this neighbourhood far behind before the authorities arrived to investigate the cause of the disturbance that must have been felt wherever scientists monitor the earth's crust for evidence of seismic activity.

It took them a couple of hours to reach the car. After a quick cup of coffee and more bread and salami, they set off north, John driving, heading away from a place neither of them ever wished to see again.

'I sure am tired of bread and salami,' George said.

'Me, too,' John responded.

They drove on a little further, accessing a wider road. Further on still, they hit a main road with signposts telling them how far they had to go to reach Lviv and Kiev.

'We did it,' George said suddenly, with what sounded like heartfelt satisfaction.

John nodded. 'We certainly did,' he replied with a reluctant grin. 'And how!'

CHAPTER FORTY-FIVE

At Lviv International airport they managed to get KLM flights leaving for Heathrow in a couple of hours.

George charged his card.

'Are you sure?' John asked. 'They're not economy prices, even if they are economy seats.'

'What do you expect, somewhere like this? No, we'll stick them on the card Ted gave me. Let his budget manager sort it out.'

They got through the formalities and headed for a lounge.

'How about a beer?' John suggested.

'Excellent idea!' George chuckled and said, 'How about two?'

John grinned. They had certainly earned it. Once settled, though, the pressure off, he wondered if George felt the same. He seemed subdued. Fatigued, probably. Exhausted. He was tired enough himself, and George had a lot more years than him to carry.

A Ukrainian language news programme was running on a nearby TV monitor. John watched it, waiting for the news the two of them could relate to most of all. Nothing appeared. He grew bored and turned away.

An announcement in several languages told them their plane was now boarding. John looked expectantly at George, who didn't seem in a hurry to respond.

'George?'

'Just thinking of poor old Ted.' Shaking his head, George said woefully, 'A lifetime of service in the national interest.'

'And then you're dead,' John fired back. 'Ain't life a bitch?'

'It sure is sweet, though,' George responded with an appreciative smile. 'And we saved a lot of lives back there.'

'Amen to that. Come on, George. Let's go home.'

From London, they flew on to Newcastle, where Sam met them in Arrivals. Their appearance seemed to take some of the strain from her face.

'All right?' she asked anxiously.

John smiled and kissed her. 'Yes,' he said. 'I've invited George to come back with us, by the way.'

'Good! Now I'll hear his side of the story, as well as what you tell me.'

'My story will be the same as John's,' George assured her. 'There won't be a cigarette paper between 'em.'

She studied their faces for a moment and then said, 'You've been through a lot together, I can tell.'

'Yes, ma'am,' George said, reaching to touch his hat. 'We sure have.'

Tired as the two of them were, that evening they gave Sam a quick rundown on their visit to Ukraine. They wouldn't have been allowed to go to bed without it. She had spent an exceedingly anxious few days waiting to hear from them.

'So, in the end, George,' Sam said slowly, still thinking about it, 'this was all down to Ted Pearson, your former boss?'

'Not all of it, but enough. Ted never left the Cold War behind. He never really accepted that Russia had changed. But it has. Perhaps not enough, but it is different now. I know that. President Obama isn't all wrong.'

They were all quiet then for a little while.

'More coffee?' Sam asked, as the silence in the room threatened to become oppressive.

'I'll get it,' John told her. 'You sit down.'

She smiled at him gratefully.

'You were the key,' George told her. 'Ted wanted those weapons out and available, but he didn't know where the depot was. Nobody did. Setting it up had been such a secret project, that no records were kept anywhere. Jack Olsson and Viktor Sirko had the knowledge, but it was lost with them.

'But somehow Ted knew Viktor Sirko's daughter also had the knowledge. He wanted her found, and he wanted to know what she knew. Then he would be able to access the depot and get the weapons out there where they could be used.'

'So with you in his sights, Sam, he went into partnership with Yugov,' John contributed. 'Yugov would do what he couldn't do himself.'

George nodded. 'That's how it was.'

'But how did he know where I was?' Sam asked.

'George has got all that worked out,' John told her with a smile.

'Not all of it,' George cautioned.

'But most of it.'

'Let's just say some of it,' George conceded.

'Well, I want to hear it,' Sam said firmly.

'As an old Cold War warrior, Ted Pearson wanted to do more to stop the Russian incursions in Ukraine. But he couldn't. The White House had made a stand, and not even Ted could go against the wishes of the President. I believe he grew very frustrated.

'But this whole thing started when the discovery was made of what had happened to my old friend, Jack Olsson. It had been a mystery for many years, and Ted took it up automatically. The department always seeks to avenge its own.

'Inquiries brought him to your doorstep. Here was this guy who had been in that same hotel in Slovakia when Jack was killed. Naturally, Ted wanted to know all about the guy. If it turned out that he had shot Jack, then he could expect a short life.

'But the usual inquiries would have come up against big gaps in the guy's history, and not a few blank walls. Then there was his wife, who didn't seem to exist at all, at least according to official records. That got him started on some serious inquiries.

'What they told him was that once upon a time, there was an Englishman working in Lviv for Viktor Sirko, and that Englishman had a thing going with Sirko's daughter. On the fateful day when the Sirko empire was hit, the two of them disappeared, never to be heard of again. Now Ted was hooked. He couldn't have let go now even if he had wanted to.'

George paused, shrugged and looked at his audience expectantly. 'You with me?'

'Oh, yes!' Sam assured him. 'Please carry on.'

'I'm a bit tired,' he said, teasing.

'Oh, you can't stop now!'

John laughed. 'I'll make some more coffee to keep you awake, George. You just carry on.'

'It's a deal. Well . . . this is guesswork, you understand? Your husband and I have put our heads together, and this is what we believe, but we can't be certain of everything at this stage.'

'Guesswork is good,' Sam assured him.

'Well, then. Learning about Olsson's death triggered Ted's memory of the long-lost arms depot in western Ukraine. It was so secret that nothing had been recorded about the location. It was off the books.

'Knowledge of it had been vested in Jack Olsson and Viktor Sirko, who had been retained to look after it and manage it. That was a miscalculation, a huge mistake! When they were gone, the knowledge was gone. Yugov had blundered, too. He had wanted the depot badly, but had inadvertently killed everybody who knew about it when he attacked Sirko's headquarters.

'But Ted must have remembered that Sirko's daughter also knew about the depot. Perhaps Sirko himself had once told him. So now Ted wanted you folks checked out properly. He still wanted Olsson's death avenged, but most of all he wanted the location and the key to the depot.

'In other words, Sam, he wanted your knowledge. He hit on the idea of using me to ferret it out, maybe by bargaining with you about the Olsson money. I don't know. And he used me because I was off the books, too. I was retired. Either that or he decided to use Yugov to get the information he needed once I had confirmed your identity.

'Yugov was already in the picture, by the way, because Ted had decided to use him to get the arms out of the depot and distributed to people who could use them effectively.'

'Wouldn't the government in Kiev have done that?'

'Not really. They would have been too squeamish about the chemical weapons. Also, the official armed forces don't seem to be worth a damn when they come up against Russian troops. The real fighting in the east is being done by irregular volunteer militias. They were the boys to get the weapons to. And Yugov would be in a good position to do that — for a price. Ted wouldn't have wanted them to be wasted.

'But things got out of control, which is what usually happens. Yugov got impatient and jumped the gun. He didn't wait for me, and then Ted, to confirm your identity and get the location of the depot. He decided he could do all that quicker himself. So he came for you, Sam.'

George paused, sipped his coffee and added, 'The rest you know.'

'Thank you, George,' Sam said gravely. After a pause, she added, 'My poor country!'

'It's in better shape than it might have been, if Ted had got away with it,' George pointed out. 'Chernobyl would have been nothing compared with what would have happened then.'

The next day, John decided this was the right time to do something about a remaining piece of unfinished business. He was surprised George hadn't mentioned it himself.

'When you go home, George, how about taking the best part of $10,000,000 with you?'

George looked at him owlishly.

'We don't need it. We don't want it, either!'

'Give it back to the US Treasury,' Sam urged. 'John's right. It has been a big problem for us for the last ten years.'

George chuckled and shook his head. 'You folks! Still, bound to be somebody in Washington who can use it! I'll see what I can do.'

The man in charge of the storage depot in Wallsend said he was very sorry. They had been on his list of people to contact, but it was such a long list he just hadn't been able to get to them yet.

'What about?' John asked.

The man waved vaguely towards a distant building on the site. 'The fire,' he said. 'The entire interior of the building was gutted. We don't know how it happened. It's still being investigated. Arson, the police think. I'm sorry. Can we talk another time about how to proceed?'

'Just a minute! You can't brush me off like this. I had important . . .'

'Leave it for now, John,' George said, touching his arm.

'What the hell do you mean — leave it!' John said, swinging round angrily. 'You know what was in there.'

'Leave it,' George said quietly, but firmly. 'Maybe it's for the best. It's over, John. You and Sam can get on with your lives now.'

It was a struggle but the anger subsided. Turning back to the man behind the desk, John said, 'We'll talk again. I'll want compensation for the . . . for the furniture I've lost.'

'Sure,' the man, bone-tired of it all, said. 'I'll put you on the list.'

'Where's home, George?' Sam asked as they got ready to take their guest to the airport.

'Vermont, these days. I have a place in the backwoods up there. You should pay me a visit someday. All of you, including the little fella there,' he said, tickling Kyle under the chin. Kyle growled in protest.

'We'd like that,' Sam assured him.

After a round of handshakes, George left them, heading off to Departures, and home.

'We won't see George again, will we?' Sam asked on the drive home.

John shook his head. 'I don't think so. Not a man like him. But we'll think of him, won't we?'

'Oh, yes,' she said. 'Every single day, probably!'

THE END

ALSO BY DAN LATUS

STANDALONES
RUN FOR HOME
AND THEN YOU'RE DEAD

JAKE ORD THRILLERS
Book 1: NO PLACE TO HIDE
Book 2: NEVER LOOK BACK
Book 3: LAST RESORT

FRANK DOY SERIES
Book 1: RISKY MISSION
Book 2: OUT OF THE NIGHT
Book 3: A DEATH AT SOUTH GARE
Book 4: LIVING DANGEROUSLY
Book 5: ONE DAMN THING AFTER ANOTHER
Book 6: SAVING HARRY
Book 7: BOROVKSY'S GOLD
Book 8: TERROR FROM THE SEA
Book 9: NOT DEAD YET

Thank you for reading this book.

If you enjoyed it please leave feedback on Amazon or Goodreads, and if there is anything we missed or you have a question about, then please get in touch. We appreciate you choosing our book.

Founded in 2014 in Shoreditch, London, we at Joffe Books pride ourselves on our history of innovative publishing. We were thrilled to be shortlisted for Independent Publisher of the Year at the British Book Awards.

www.joffebooks.com

We're very grateful to eagle-eyed readers who take the time to contact us. Please send any errors you find to corrections@joffebooks.com. We'll get them fixed ASAP.

www.ingramcontent.com/pod-product-compliance
Lightning Source LLC
Chambersburg PA
CBHW021957190626
46808CB00017B/2115